HOLIDAY DREAMS

HOLIDAY DREAMS

•

Annette Mahon

AVALON BOOKS
NEW YORK

Published by Thomas Bouregy & Co., Inc.
160 Madison Avenue, New York, NY 10016

Library of Congress Cataloging-in-Publication Data

Mahon, Annette.
    Holiday dreams / Annette Mahon.
        p. cm.
    ISBN 978-0-8034-9923-2 (acid-free paper)   1. Quilts—
Fiction.   2. Hawaii—Fiction.   I. Title.

    PS3563.A3595H65   2008
    813'.54—dc22   2008023051

PRINTED IN THE UNITED STATES OF AMERICA
ON ACID-FREE PAPER
BY HADDON CRAFTSMEN, BLOOMSBURG, PENNSYLVANIA

For Nathan and Kira: *me ke aloha pumehana.*

Note to reader:
"Momi" is the Hawaiian word for pearl.
It is also a popular name for women.
The proper pronunciation is: moé-mee.

Chapter One

Momi pounded on the door of apartment number one, the apartment with the discreet little sign reading MANAGER above the bell. Pushing the bell had gotten her nowhere, so she was now beating on the door with her fists, leaving damp, circular smudges with each touch.

"Come on, answer," she muttered under her breath. Then she gathered herself for another shout. "Help! I've got an emergency upstairs." All the while she continued hammering on the door.

When the door finally opened, it happened so quickly that Momi, with her fist still up and ready, almost fell forward into the arms of the man who'd opened it. Catching her balance just before it became necessary for him to rescue her, she straightened to her full height and glared at him.

"Didn't you hear me? I've got an emergency upstairs."

"Lady, I'm surprised the fire department rescue truck isn't here, with all the noise you're making."

Momi glowered. But she also saw the man for the first time. Really saw him. He was as wet as she was. And not wearing a shirt. Damp blue jeans covered his lower half. Nothing but a scattering of damp brown hairs covered his expansive chest, tanned to a deep, golden brown.

Momi swallowed. Dragging her reluctant gaze back to his face, she managed to find her voice. "You were in the shower."

"Ten points to the wet lady."

She found herself staring at his chest again and forced her eyes upward, just in time to catch his eyes scanning her wet figure in a way that made her blush.

"I usually take off my clothes before I shower," he said.

His wry grin might have been attractive if she hadn't been so wet and so angry. But before she could sputter out a reply—or a put-down—he continued.

"I guess you have some kind of plumbing emergency."

Momi grit her teeth. "Ten points to the damp gentleman."

"Oh, lady, I'm no gentleman."

The grin he proffered brought out a deep dimple in his left cheek. A shiver created gooseflesh up her arms, and Momi knew he noticed. She rubbed her hands quickly back and forth over her arms.

"It's getting cold," she murmured.

And that was a lie, pure and simple, she admitted to

herself. If she wasn't so wet and so upset, she could actually go for this rude older man, Momi thought. He wasn't classically handsome, but that roguish grin was melting even her chilly heart. And that thought made her madder than ever.

She threw him a fierce scowl that appeared to affect him not at all.

"If it's such an emergency, we'd better get up there," he said.

But Momi was having trouble getting past that bare chest. What was wrong with her? This was Kona, Hawaii, for gosh sakes. She'd seen her share of bare male chests, and she'd never reacted with more than an appreciative grin.

She swallowed, trying to moisten a dry throat, and shivered again. Her throat was probably the only part of her that was dry. She needed to get back to her place; a tall glass of water was definitely in order.

She stepped back quickly when she realized that the bare chest before her was getting closer. Her startled eyes looked into his face.

"Aren't you going to get dressed?"

Her question brought another wide grin, flashing that dimple yet again. This time her heart did a little skip. He had absolutely amazing green eyes. They were just the color of peridot, the "Hawaiian diamonds" found in the black sand that covered so many Big Island beaches. And they twinkled with mischief—and promise. Just like the dimple that was making her heart flutter.

"I am dressed."

Momi gave up. There was no purpose to arguing with someone who must think he was God's gift to women. She didn't like him, and she absolutely didn't like the way she was reacting to him.

Without another word, Momi turned and mounted the steps.

She fumed all the way up. This was supposed to be her big night. She was due at a Halloween party at the Orchid House Resort, a party hosted by her brother-in-law, the general manager there. Momi had dressed carefully in a red flapper dress decorated with fringe. She'd saved it particularly for the party tonight, wearing a witch's black dress and hat to the library for the children's party she'd held that afternoon. She'd wanted a "wow" look for the big party and thought she'd found it in the slinky red dress. The fringe moved temptingly when she did, the lowest row at the hem dancing becomingly a few inches above her knees. Strappy, spike-heeled red sandals and a sequined, feathered headband completed the look.

And now this! She was dripping wet, her hair and dress ruined, and the jaunty feather drooped limply against her forehead. She didn't know what her makeup looked like, either, and she'd spent a full half hour getting it just right. Natural-looking. It took a lot of work to achieve that no-makeup look.

Now she wondered if she'd even get to the party tonight. How long would it take Macho Man to fix the faucet, and what on earth would she wear if she did go? And whatever could she do with her hair?

Rick followed the seething tenant up the stairs. And a pretty sight it was, too, following the dripping woman. The sweet little flapper dress she wore was wet enough to leave drops of water in her path, and it clung very nicely to her full curves. Climbing the stairs behind that gently swaying derriere was no hardship. In fact, he was sorry to reach the landing. Some men might admire the skeletal look so popular among models and movie stars, but he'd always preferred a woman with a fuller figure. Some nice curves to fill his palms—that was what he liked, and she definitely had those. Dramatic flair was another quality he admired, and she had that too. He wouldn't have been surprised to see steam rising from her head—she was that mad. And wouldn't that be a simple way to dry off her dress?

Her apartment was the one right over his, the upstairs front corner. Momi Kanahele, children's librarian at the public library just a few blocks away, had moved in July first with the help of numerous locals he assumed were relatives. There had been hours of stomping around up there that day, but she'd been pretty quiet since.

If he hadn't been in the shower, he might have heard some commotion this evening, though. He would bet she hadn't taken that soaking quietly. Just think, she'd been directly above him when it had happened. Amazing that her rage hadn't traveled past the running water and alerted him, just a few feet below her.

He followed her across the living area to the bathroom, the obvious source of the problem. The carpet just outside the bathroom door was darker than the rest, heavy with water. It made squishing noises as they walked over it—he in bare feet, she in the sexiest shoes he'd ever seen. Red straps crossed her toes and instep, wrapping around trim ankles. Spike heels showed off the muscles of her legs, making them worth a second or even third look.

"So, what seems to be the problem?"

Actually, Rick could see immediately what had happened. But he liked the way she looked when she was irate. The way she looked right now. Her eyebrows shot upward, widening her large eyes even more. They were a deep chocolate brown—and not wimpy milk chocolate, but the deep, rich color of semisweet. He couldn't even see the pupils, the irises were so dark. A limp red feather wilted in her hair, sagging downward from a glittery headband to land just to the right of her left eye. Another casualty of the leak, he assumed.

He saw her take a deep breath—just after stealing a quick peek at his chest. Then she swallowed hard.

Well, well. The little librarian was intimidated by a bare chest. Such a cliché! He could feel his lips twitch as he fought a smile. *Her* lips, he noticed, were pulled tight.

"I went to turn on the faucet to wash my hands. And the handle just broke right off."

Her voice became shrill as she finished, picking up the offending object and gesturing with it.

"Just came right off, and water shot up all over me, the room—everywhere! It's ruined my makeup," she added, gesturing at several compacts, tubes, and pencils lying on the counter. Everything was soaked, and water pooled inside a container of pink blush.

He couldn't resist glancing down her damp figure once more. It was a sight worth seeing, that was certain. The thin fabric of her costume let every little thing show now that it was wet.

"You knew about the shut-off valve."

"Yes, I knew about the shut-off valve. And lucky for you that I did. Otherwise, you'd have water running down the stairs by now, not to mention dripping down your apartment's walls."

He nodded, taking the faucet handle from her. "I'll get on it first thing in the morning. But I have to warn you, there may be more involved than just replacing this bit." He held up the broken piece of chrome. "The plumbing in this building is old, and when something like this happens, I usually have to replace everything."

She didn't look happy, but she did nod.

"So you'll have to use the kitchen for teeth-brushing for a couple of days."

"A couple of days? I thought you said you'd get right on it."

"I will. But in case you didn't notice, it's Halloween. I have to stay around downstairs tonight to discourage pranksters. I also said it might involve more than replacing this one piece. If I can't get parts, it could take a day or two to replace everything. I just want you to be prepared."

Momi frowned mightily but nodded again.

"Okay. But what about the other damage? Look at this place!"

The bathroom was a soggy mess. The shower curtain, striped in shades of blue, pulled at the hooks, heavy with water. Who had a cloth shower curtain? What a dumb idea, he thought, though he saw that there was a plastic liner behind it. She also had baskets of towels and soaps and shells on the counter and toilet back—most of them now full of water. A navy oval rug was so wet, water squeezed out around his toes when he stepped on it. Blue water.

"And what about my clothes? This dress is completely ruined. Is the landlord going to pay to replace it?"

There was a catch in her voice that made his heart lurch. Trying to ignore it, he returned to the saucy tone he'd adopted earlier. "Hot date tonight?"

She glared at him. "Not that it's any of your business, but I'm going to my sister's. Her husband is general manager of the Orchid House Resort, and this is a big, important party for her. I can't arrive there like this. I look like a drowned rat."

The last words were almost a wail.

"Well, it is a unique costume idea."

His deadpan delivery earned him nothing more than another glare.

"Maybe you could be a *Titanic* survivor?" he tried, hoping to coax a smile from her.

Her response was to ignore him.

"This party is important to my sister," she repeated.

Rick thought she looked ready to cry. And if there was anything he hated, it was a crying woman.

He walked quickly out of the bathroom and around the corner into the bedroom. Momi followed, almost nipping his bare heels with her bright red toenails.

"What are you *doing*?" she asked, irritation mixed with anger in her voice.

"I'll bet you have something right here that will work for a costume."

Heading toward the closet, he stopped abruptly as he spotted a pile of black fabric on the bed, topped with a peaked witch's hat.

"What's this? A witch costume? What's wrong with this?" Pushing the hat aside, he grabbed the dress, holding it up by the shoulders.

"I wore that all day at work," Momi replied. "I wanted something special for my sister's party." Her voice broke on the final words, and she sniffed heavily.

Uh-oh, Rick thought. She was going to cry after all.

He dropped the witch costume back onto the bed and yanked open the closet doors.

"What are you *doing*?" Momi cried once again, her voice rising along with the emphasis on the final word. She was almost shouting.

She was mad now, but at least she didn't look ready

to cry, Rick thought as he flung the hangers along the rod, quickly looking over and assessing each item of clothing.

"Being the apartment manager does *not* give you the right to go through my closet," Momi protested.

But it was Rick's turn to ignore her. "My friends and I never bought anything special for Halloween," he said, "and we always managed."

"This is a big, important party." Momi sniffed.

Good Lord, she wasn't crying, was she?

With a feeling of relief, he pulled a long dress from the back of the closet.

"Here it is. Wear this."

Momi was staring at him, her mouth open, her eyes blazing. Okay, so he'd invaded her space. He couldn't let her cry because she couldn't go to some silly costume party, could he? And yelling at him wasn't going to fix her ruined dress.

"My hula costume?"

"Is that what this is?" He shrugged. It was a long dress, satin, pink. Looked like a costume to him. "See? It's already a costume."

She frowned mightily, but at least she wasn't arguing. And she no longer looked ready to cry.

"I'd need some leis. And my hair . . ."

Her hands went up to her damp hair. It was piled on her head, pins poking out of it, wisps flying out, creating a halolike affect. The red band helped contain it, and he wondered how it had looked before she was drenched.

Because he liked it just the way it was, limp feather and all. He especially liked the two long corkscrew curls hanging down her neck.

He shoved the hanger at her, surprised when she leaped backward.

"Watch it!" she said. "Satin can't get wet!"

"Sure, it can." He grinned again.

She almost grinned back this time—he was sure of it.

"Yeah, and it will be ruined, just like this dress," she said, gesturing toward her clothing.

He didn't want to look at her wet dress again, or he'd be too distracted. Instead, he tossed the hanger, dress and all, across the bed. Momi gasped as the shiny pink fabric slid across the quilt, then began to slide toward the edge of the bed. Just in time, the hook of the hanger caught in a fold of the black cotton witch dress. The slide toward the floor was halted, not that Rick could see why there would be a problem if it did pool on the floor for a second or two. It wasn't wet in here.

However, he heard Momi release her breath in a swoosh, so he knew she had worried about that. There was just no accounting for the way a woman's mind worked.

Still, he was responsible for apartment maintenance, so you could say her costume problem was his fault. Indirectly. And he hated to be the cause of her disappointment. He could see how upset she was about everything, even if he did think it was all a lot of ridiculousness.

"You put this on," he said, gesturing toward the pink dress, "and fix your hair. I'll go get you a couple of leis."

Before she had time to object to the way he was taking over, he strode purposefully from the room. There was a flower shop just down the street, and he could probably get there and back in fifteen minutes. It would be closed, but he knew the owner, knew she lived upstairs. She was sure to have something suitable left in her shop's stock.

A smile appeared as he tripped down the steps. He'd get the leis. Then she'd owe him one. It never hurt to have a lovely woman in your debt.

Momi watched the manager leave without even a good-bye. The nerve of him, going through her closet.

Momi glanced at the pink satin *holokū* he'd tossed across the bed. She hadn't worn it in years, but she thought it would still fit. And it was a beautiful dress. If she could do something with her hair . . . And if he showed up with the leis . . . It wasn't her beautiful flapper dress, but, well, things happened. She sighed.

As she stepped closer to the bed, her glance moved from the pink satin to the red and white Hawaiian quilt covering her bed. Her breath caught in her throat as she thought of what might have happened if the heirloom quilt had gotten wet. No, she wouldn't even consider that. It was too horrible for even wordless thoughts.

Beautiful but very old, the quilt was one of the reasons she was so determined to attend Jade's party tonight. The quilt was a family heirloom, passed from mother to daughter in her mother's family. Her family was the first in all that time to have more than one daughter, so it had come to her from her older sister. Family legend claimed that the owner of the quilt would meet her true love soon after receiving it. And Momi had been given the quilt just the week before, during her twenty-fourth birthday celebration. She and her last boyfriend had drifted apart during her final year of graduate school, and she was more than ready for a new relationship.

Peeling off the wet, probably ruined, red flapper dress, Momi allowed herself a deep sigh. She'd planned so carefully, asking her mother to help her make the dress in the week she'd had available before Halloween. It had been so flattering, both in style and color. She so wanted to look her best, in this, her first social outing since receiving the quilt.

Momi looked over at the pale pink of the *holokū*. She hoped it wouldn't make her look pale and washed out. With her light brown skin, she really looked best in bright, primary colors like carmine red and sapphire blue. She wasn't so sure about the carnation pink, but at this point she had little choice.

Clad in a fresh set of dry underwear, Momi went into the bathroom to see what she could do about her hair. Just in time, she realized that she shouldn't plug in the hair dryer in the wet room.

Mumbling under her breath, she moved back into the

bedroom, dryer in hand. She had to crouch down a little to make it work, but she didn't have time to search out an extension cord. She'd blow it until it was mostly dry. Luckily, wearing what amounted to a hula costume meant she could wear her hair down; long and kinky would fit right in with the hula look.

Momi was just pulling up the zipper of the *holokū* when she heard the manager call out. From *inside* the apartment!

One arm still around her torso as she attempted to reach the last few inches of the zipper closure, Momi stormed into the living room. The manager stood there, a long white box in his hands. At least he'd managed to find a shirt to wear, even if it was old and faded.

"Haven't you heard of knocking? How dare you just walk in here like that? I might not have been decent."

He grinned at her—a real devil of a grin—as he took a long, slow look that brought a blush to her cheeks.

"One can only hope."

Darn. She wanted to stay angry at him, but he did have the most engaging eyes. And his dimple!

She took a deep breath. She supposed that his ribald remark was a compliment of sorts. But she was determined not to let him know how close he was to charming her.

So, ignoring his comment, she eyed the florist's box in his hands. "You found something? I hope it matches the pink," she added.

His eyebrows shot upward.

"A thank-you might be nice."

Instead of handing her the box, he put it down on the table and crossed the floor to her. She noticed he was still barefoot. Had he walked to the store in his bare feet? Or had he adopted the island custom of removing his shoes at the door? It was obvious that he was from the mainland. His voice easily gave him away. Islanders might have light brown hair like his, with blond streaks she felt sure were naturally bestowed by the sun. But she'd never seen an islander with eyes that color, and his voice was a dead giveaway. A Californian, perhaps? A surfer boy grown into a beach bum?

She was still wondering where he'd come from and what he was doing managing an apartment complex in Kona when he stepped behind her. Pushing her hand aside, he gently lifted her long hair to rest over her shoulders, then quickly pulled the zipper up the rest of the way, even taking care of the hook at the top of the closure.

"What are you doing?" She turned quickly, slapping at his hands.

It didn't faze him in the least. He merely gave her another of his teasing grins, flashing that darned dimple at her.

"I would think it was fairly obvious. I saw that it was hard for you to reach those last few inches. But would you like me to open it up for you again so you can do it yourself?"

Momi quickly increased the distance between them.

She had no doubt he *would* undo the zipper if she scolded him for his overfamiliarity.

She was determined to be polite, since he had helped her, but she looked pointedly at her watch. "I'm really late. Did you get any leis?"

"I said I would, and I always deliver or my promises." He stepped toward the white box.

"I'll keep that in mind about the plumbing."

She'd spoken quietly, but he heard her.

"Eventually," he added, as he tossed aside the top of the box.

Momi might have argued, but she saw what he lifted from the tissue before she could get out any sarcastic words. And then they all died on her tongue. Because what he'd brought for her was so perfect, she could hardly believe he was a *haole*. Maybe he'd lived here longer than she supposed. Or maybe he was just lucky.

"Oh, they're beautiful!"

She reached eagerly for the blossoms—several long strings of crown flowers intertwined with fragrant *maile*. They would be perfect with the *holokū*. If the dress was white, she'd look like a bride.

The thought brought back her hopes and dreams about the evening's party. She just had to get over to the hotel.

But the manager—she never did get his name, she realized—wasn't making it easy. He continued to hold on to the lei.

She finally voiced her exasperation. "What?"

He had to be the most frustrating man on earth! Why, oh, why did all this have to happen to her tonight?

"I have to put it on you," he insisted. "Isn't that the way it works?"

With a sigh, Momi stepped forward. He was right, of course. He was giving her the lei—at least, he'd better not charge her for it. So he should put it on her. And give her a kiss. A lei was given in the spirit of aloha. It was a gift of warmth, of hospitality, of love. Although in this particular case, Momi thought it was given in . . . what? Friendship? Their meeting had not been under the best of circumstances; he probably just meant to apologize for his earlier boorish behavior.

Just a kiss on the cheek, she thought.

It had better be on the cheek!

Rick stepped right up to Momi, stopping just short of invading her personal space. He could tell from the way she'd acted so far that she would not like it if he got too close. But, hey, this was his right, and he sure planned to take advantage. Otherwise, she could darn well pay the exorbitant price he'd been charged for the flowers.

Still looking into her face, he grasped the lei gently in both hands and lifted it over her head.

She had a lovely face. Those dark, dark eyes—cat eyes that tilted up at the outside corners in a most intriguing manner. Long, long lashes that curled upward in a thick sweep of deep brown. And the most beautiful skin he'd ever seen. It looked as smooth and soft as a silk stocking. A strange analogy, perhaps, but the first one that came to him. One of his earliest memories was of being scolded for touching his mother's silk stockings. He'd ruin them, she'd told him. Good little boys did not play with ladies' stockings.

Casting aside that ancient memory, Rick lowered the lei over Momi's head, letting it rest on her shoulders. Carefully he took her hair in his hands and lifted it free of the flowers. He was surprised to find it as soft and silky as he imagined her skin to be; it looked rough and bristly, curling wildly around her face.

Finally he placed his hands lightly on her shoulders and leaned forward, inhaling the heady aroma of the *maile* as he placed a gentle kiss on her lips.

Her lips were as soft as he'd imagined, and he wanted to taste her too. He knew she'd be sweet, but he also knew that that would be going too far. He'd already pushed things by kissing her lips. He knew she'd expected a peck on the cheek. But what fun would that be?

Stepping back, Rick waited for a tongue-lashing. He loved the way her eyes flashed when she was angry. A half smile played at his lips while he imagined the taste of her on them. There did seem to be something on his lips—a quick taste of sweetness that he couldn't quite identify.

But surprise, surprise. The lady was staring at him with a strange look on her face that he was at a loss to interpret. Surprise? Horror? Odd. He'd been reading her easily before this.

Finally coming out of what was almost a trance, he saw her lift her hands up to her hair, running her fingers through the curls and lifting them in some type of female preening action. She then hurried into the bedroom to check her appearance in the mirror. He could see her continue to fuss with her hair as he stood in the doorway. Not wanting to push her any further that evening, he was keeping his distance.

"It looks great," he said.

She turned a quizzical look toward him. "It does. How did you know?" The slight purple tinge of the crown flowers blended with the pink of her dress, creating the perfect complement. There was such a deep question in her voice, he had to laugh.

"What? Guys can't choose flowers?"

He was sure he saw color bloom in her cheeks.

"They can. But they aren't usually very good at it."

She gave him a speculative look that made him laugh even harder.

"And you're not even a *kamaʻāina*. Are you?"

No, he wasn't. But he knew the word. A native.

"I've lived here awhile," he replied.

That was apparently enough for Momi. She suddenly remembered that she was in a tremendous hurry, scooping up her purse and car keys.

Rick, however, wasn't quite done. "There's more," he told her, returning to the other room to retrieve the white floral box. "Kalani—she's the florist two doors down—included these. In case you wanted something for your hair." He parted the tissue, revealing three stargazer lilies.

"Oh!" Momi breathed out the word as she saw the beautiful pink flowers, inhaling their heady perfume at the same time.

She dropped her things onto the table beside the box, her keys clattering as they hit the wooden surface.

"They're wonderful. Even better than a head lei."

She reached for the flowers, starting into the bathroom but catching herself in time to detour to the bedroom before the train of her *holokū* became wet.

From the doorway, Rick watched her clip the stems of the large lilies, then take her glorious hair and twist it loosely up on top of her head. She retrieved a clip of some sort from the top of her dresser to fasten it all there, then pinned the lilies into place. He'd often seen the local women wearing giant blossoms in their hair; it was a style made popular by the hula groups, he'd heard. He did notice that the dancing girls often had their hair up with clusters of enormous flowers pinned in, like some variation of the Vegas showgirl headdress. It amazed him how they could manage it. And now he saw how effortless it was to Momi. Within minutes she was done, fluffing her hair and tucking in a piece here and there.

Rick had to swallow a lump in his throat, surprising himself by the intensity of his feeling for this woman. She had become so fired up over her accidental dousing. Was she as zealous about other things? Her work? The environment? Boyfriends? And holidays, he thought with a frown, as he noted the abundance of Halloween decorations that graced the apartment.

And that reminded him to back off. He didn't do holidays. Halloween led to Thanksgiving, which led inevitably to Christmas. And for sure, Rick did not do Christmas.

Solemn now, he watched her rush out of the bedroom, grab her things, and head for the door. And despite his self-warning, Rick had to grin. She'd yelled at him for entering her apartment without knocking, but now she seemed to forget that he was there. He heard the door lock and her footsteps move down the steps.

Within minutes the footsteps returned. The key sounded in the lock.

Momi opened the door, a frown once again gracing her face. Her eyes flashed. She did look a treat when she was angry.

"Will you be starting the cleanup right away?"

Rick knew he ought to say "of course," but he couldn't resist another challenge. "As soon as I check out the damage and go down for my keys. So I can lock up when I leave," he added.

Momi's eyes turned friendlier. She might be quick-tempered, but it seemed she forgave easily too.

"Thanks, uh . . ."

Momi stared at him, and Rick could almost see her shifting through mental files for something. He quickly realized what it must be.

"It's Rick."

She grinned at him, and you'd have thought she'd reached out and touched him. His chest flooded with warmth.

"Thanks, Rick. *A hui hou!*" she called out, rushing down the steps.

See you later, Rick translated. Yeah, he'd see her later, all right. He looked forward to it.

Chapter Two

"**M**omi, you looked fantastic tonight."

It was after midnight, and Jade and Momi sat amid a cocoon of pillows on the queen-sized bed in Jade's guest room. Weeks ago she'd suggested that Momi spend the night with them after the Halloween party. Momi had planned to return to her own apartment, but after the events of the early evening, she'd reconsidered.

After changing into their nightclothes, the two sisters made themselves comfortable in the big bed, combing each other's hair and generally acting like the children they'd once been.

"But what happened to that flapper dress I heard so much about?"

Momi sighed. She'd arrived at her sister's party late, said a quick hello to her host and hostess, and joined right in. For the first time in her life, she'd made an entrance, and now she realized why some women planned late arrivals. It was a heady feeling, walking into the room and having all eyes turn to her. To see the smiles and admiring glances bestowed on her by the men.

Momi groaned. "I'm trying to forget. I'm sure it's ruined. I had a flood in my bathroom."

In dramatic fashion, she told her story, emphasizing the wetness of her clothing and the rudeness of the apartment manager.

"The dress was a mess," she finally said, heaving a giant sigh. "I still can't believe it. It looked so darn good until I got drenched."

"Well, wearing the *holokū* was a great idea," Jade said. "Everyone was talking about how great you looked. Even Adam said 'Wow' when you walked in."

Momi smiled. "I hope you elbowed him in the ribs for that."

"Oh, don't worry, I know he just likes to look. He wouldn't be human if he didn't, right? I don't mind."

Jade looked so peaceful and content that Momi felt a pang of jealousy. She wanted that for herself.

"I didn't actually choose the *holokū*," she admitted. "I was wailing about my ruined costume and the big, important party I was invited to, and Rick walked right into my bedroom and started going through my closet. Can you imagine?"

"Rick is the manager who came up to fix the faucet? And he found that dress?" Jade waved a hand toward the room's closet, where the pink satin of the *holokū* shimmered in the shadows.

Momi nodded. "It was a hula costume, and I don't even know why I kept it. Except that it is a beautiful dress."

"What about the leis and flowers? Your hair looked terrific, you know. I love stargazer lilies."

"Rick—and, yes, that's the apartment manager's name—said he'd get me a lei, and he did. He apparently went to a florist shop two doors from the apartment building and got them from the woman there. He said she was the one who thought of including the lilies for my hair."

She wrapped her hands around her bent legs, lay her cheek against one knee, and sighed. "My hair did look nice, didn't it? It got so frizzy from being soaked, I wasn't sure I'd be able to do anything with it. So pulling it up like that worked great. The lilies were a perfect complement to the dress. I'll have to stop in there tomorrow. . . ." Momi paused as she turned to look at the bedside alarm clock. "I'll have to stop in there later to-day," she amended, "and thank her for them. It was nice of her to think of it."

Jade laughed. "Well, the manager probably paid her for them, don't you think? You should probably thank him when you get back. Also for the success of your last-minute costume."

Momi's startled expression showed that she hadn't thought of that. Still, Rick was at least partially responsible for her first costume's being destroyed. If he kept the place in top condition, the faucets wouldn't become geysers, would they?

But her conscience wouldn't let her dismiss his help. She would have to thank him. Perhaps even offer to pay for the flowers. He didn't look as if he could afford to pay for expensive flowers. The few times she'd seen him before the previous evening, he'd been dressed in clothes that looked like they came from the Salvation Army's resale shop. Not that *she* could afford the extra expense either, but at least she had a real job.

"Anyway," Jade continued, "he sounds like a resourceful guy. And that's probably a good thing in an apartment manager. Is he fixing the damage as we speak?"

"I sure hope so."

"Well, you looked terrific. Everyone thought so. Did you see the way the guys gawked at you when you walked in? You definitely need to thank this Rick."

"Yeah. Right after I thank him for fixing my faucet," Momi said, a deep frown marring her earlier cheery countenance. "I was furious with him at first. I was so looking forward to this party, and I'd planned what I would wear so carefully. And then to have it all ruined like that in just a few seconds."

She shook her head. "I am so ready for a new relationship. It's been months since I had a date. Josh and I just drifted apart while I was in graduate school. He was working odd hours, and I was studying . . . and pretty soon we were going weeks between dates. Then months." She shook her head, still uncertain about just how she and her longtime beau had broken up.

Then she gave a bright, hopeful grin. "But now I have the Lovell quilt, and I'm expecting great things." She winked at her sister. "Look at the wonderful man Great-great-grandmother Helen found for you."

Momi couldn't help noticing the satisfied expression on Jade's face, the complete contentment she'd found since meeting the right man and becoming a happily married woman.

"You met a lot of guys tonight."

"Yes, I did." Momi frowned. She'd expected the powerful *mana* of her ancestor to bring flashing lights and ringing bells—or at least a rainbow. But there had been none of that. The men she'd met had been nice, polite, good dance partners. But none of them seemed to be that special someone.

"How long was it after Mom gave you the quilt before you met Adam?"

"I met him right away," Jade said. Her face glowed with an inner happiness as she recalled their initial meeting. "Mom gave me the quilt one afternoon, and I attended a reception at the hotel the following evening. And there he was."

Momi sighed. "I guess Mom did say it's always worked quickly." Fast was good, but if she'd already met the man of her dreams, she wanted to be in on it. "So, do you think one of the men I met tonight is him?"

"Only you can know, Momi," Jade replied. "I sure

didn't think Adam was the one. Of course, my scientist's mind didn't really believe in the quilt, remember? I was shocked that Mom seemed to put her faith in such superstitious nonsense. You were the one who was sure it would work the way Mom claimed. You even suggested Adam might be the one, and I was still skeptical."

"I do believe in the quilt." Momi nodded for emphasis. "So, there were no bells ringing or stars exploding, huh?"

Jade's laughter was her answer.

"Though . . ." Jade paused. "I used to get this strange tingling at the nape of my neck whenever Adam was around. I'd almost forgotten." Her eyes turned dreamy with the memory. "It was like some kind of radar, letting me know he was there. I'd get this funny feeling at the back of my neck—kind of like an itch, but not quite— and I'd look around, and there he was."

"That's so romantic." Momi sighed. "I didn't feel anything tonight. With any of the guys, even though they were all nice and I had a good time. A couple of them asked if they could call. I guess I'll just have to wait and see."

"Try to relax. The quilt has worked for four generations of Lovell women so far. I'm sure it will work for you too."

It was approaching noon when Momi returned to her apartment. The rain that had started in the early-morning hours had become a misty drizzle; the skies remained gray, and the humid air felt thick and sticky. Luckily, Jade had provided a plastic dry-cleaner's bag to protect her pink satin *holokū*. She would have to have it cleaned after wearing it for the party, but at least it wouldn't have water stains on it.

Her apartment remained a disaster area. All the optimistic thoughts she'd tried to hold as she drove back from Jade's hadn't helped at all. In addition, a damp, musty smell now pervaded the entire suite of rooms. And the whole place had been disarranged. It was a mess.

The whir of a fan competed with the striking of raindrops on the roof as she entered; the rain was starting up in earnest again. Neither the fan nor the rain seemed to help with the smell, however, and she scrunched up her nose in distaste. And the open windows and blowing fan made the room cold and damp—much colder than the outside temperature.

Momi stood inside the door, shivering slightly and totally discouraged. What on earth had happened to her lovely apartment? All the pleasant thoughts in the world couldn't help with this situation, she thought. Besides the temperature and the unpleasant smell, someone—and she suspected Rick—had pushed all her furniture toward the counter that separated the living room and kitchen. Chairs were piled on top of the dining table, her coffee table upended on top of the sofa. All of the Halloween decorations she'd worked so hard on had been gathered up and dumped in a heap on the kitchen counter.

She looked around, hoping her eyes were playing

tricks and it wasn't as bad as she imagined. The pile of furniture also blocked access to her kitchen, an important room in any house. She'd better have water in her bathroom sink if she couldn't even get into the kitchen.

Momi's mouth tightened as she took it all in. It had to be the work of the manager, Rick—what was his last name, anyway? She planned to contact whoever was above him in the hierarchy and complain.

And where on earth was Rick? The rooms were quiet except for the sound of the rain, and Momi thought that replacing pipes would be noisy work. Shouldn't he be here? Shouldn't he be working on her plumbing?

The only thing she could see that he'd accomplished— besides creating the mess in the living room and kitchen—was the fan set in the bathroom doorway and blowing out across the living room carpet. Shedding her rubber slippers at the door, Momi stepped forward and dabbed at the carpet with her big toe. Still wet. No longer oozing water when stepped on, but still good and wet.

She heaved another sigh. Nothing was going to be easy about this situation.

She was ready to storm out the door and down the steps, shouting for Rick, but first she had to hang up her dress. As she stepped into the bedroom doorway, she collided with the object of her stressed thoughts.

He was in her bedroom?

Momi stepped back, her thoughts swirling even more than before. What was he doing in her bedroom? The water hadn't gotten that far.

Anger, white and hot, surged through her at the thought of him in her private space. She grasped the dress to her. The plastic crinkled loudly, adding to the whirring of the fan and the *pings* of raindrops hitting the roof. The faint trill of a siren added to the cacophony, and Momi thought it appropriate. Perhaps an ambulance could come right now and carry her off before she had a nervous breakdown. All this mess, just as she was looking forward to the holidays and all the fun she would have. The holidays were her favorite time of year, and this year she had her very own place to decorate, as well as the added potential of meeting her true love.

Her stomach rolled, and her fingers fisted into the thin plastic.

On the other hand, maybe the siren indicated a police car. She could just kill this smiling idiot right now and let them take her away. Was self-preservation the same as self-defense? The strange feelings that overran her whenever she saw Rick scared her. She didn't like him. He was aggravation personified. And yet here she was, getting sick to her stomach over the guy.

Momi gritted her teeth as he greeted her as though nothing out of the ordinary had happened.

"Good morning." He flashed a wide grin that showcased even, white teeth. The dimple appeared, a deep slash in his left cheek.

What nerve, Momi thought. He messes up her place, goes into her bedroom without permission, then has the gall to be cheerful?

"What's good about it?"

His eyebrows flew up, and the grin—and dimple—disappeared.

"My, we are grumpy. Are you always this way in the morning, or did you party too much last night? Hungover, are we?"

"We," she said, emphasizing the word and frowning mightily at the same time, "will be fine and dandy once *we* know what is going on here."

She gripped the dress more snugly to her, and the crinkle of the plastic was strangely comforting. It was a familiar sound in a newly unfamiliar environment. She had to hold on to the anger she felt, because otherwise she might just sit on the damp floor and cry.

Rick's eyes looked from her face to the plastic-covered dress she still clasped to her chest and back up again.

"How was the party? Was your costume suitable?"

Momi almost didn't reply, until she realized that she owed him a thank-you for his suggestion and flowers the previous evening. She'd have been in a real bind if he hadn't taken it upon himself to delve into her closet and uncover the hula costume. She'd forgotten it was even there.

And then there were the flowers.

"It was a nice party, thank you. And the costume worked very well. Thank you for suggesting it and for getting the flowers."

She tried to smile, but it was difficult. She was still

upset about finding her apartment in such a disheveled condition.

"Do I need to reimburse you for the flowers?" she added. She didn't want to come right out and ask if he could afford the expense, and this seemed the appropriate time to bring in a casual mention of payment.

Rick grinned at her statement, as though he was completely responsible for her success at the party. He didn't seem to notice the reluctance in her thank-you. Well, he might be the one to credit, but it was hard for her to admit it. Just as it was difficult for her to admit to herself how appealing he looked when he grinned that way.

"You don't have to pay me for the flowers. You can consider it a gift from management after the inconvenience you had to endure."

Momi was pleasantly surprised. She started to thank him but was stopped by his next words.

"I also took that red dress you hung over the shower rail last night to the cleaners to see if they can do anything with it."

"Th-thank you."

Momi fought a mixture of shame and delight. He wasn't helping her deal with the unreasonable attraction she felt—not when he insisted on being nice. That little half smile he gave her with his words—good grief, how could anyone ignore that? Her heart pounded, its rate easily twice its normal beat.

What was it about him? Not his sartorial elegance. His clothing was old and worn, his posture poor. He slouched instead of standing tall, reminding her of teenage boys she saw hanging around the library trying to look cool. Besides that, he sorely needed a shave. A lot of women liked that scruffy look, but she never had.

So how could he look so . . . so . . . yummy?

As her eyes met his, her heart skipped a beat, maybe two, then started up again at an even more accelerated rate. His eyes were amazing, of course, but that alone couldn't affect her heart rate or send her temperature soaring. The clear green was almost unbelievable. If he wasn't such a casual dresser, she'd think he wore colored contacts. But why would someone who didn't bother with his clothes or his appearance bother to get colored contacts?

She frowned as she continued to stare into his eyes. No, it wasn't the color alone that drew her. There was life in his eyes—a twinkle of mischief, a hint of amusement. And the fine lines that bracketed them bestowed character.

Her gaze still locked with his, she found herself unable to move as his hand reached toward her. Light as a butterfly's touch, his fingers trailed over the furrows marring her forehead.

"You don't want to frown like that."

His soft voice insinuated itself into her pores.

"You'll get wrinkles."

His voice was so considerate, so caring, Momi found herself drawn to him, leaning forward into his touch.

Until she realized what she was doing and pulled

back into a rigidly upright position. The plastic covering her dress crinkled noisily.

Frustrated by troublesome thoughts and even more troublesome feelings, Momi resorted once more to anger.

"Why is my place such a mess? And *what* were you doing in my bedroom?"

Rick almost smiled at the indignation pulling Momi's lips into a tight line. Her forehead smoothed out as her eyebrows flew upward and her nostrils flared. It wouldn't surprise him at all if sparks flew from her eyes.

She sure was cute when she was upset. Not that he'd intended to upset her. Pushing all the furniture aside was to help dry out the carpet. And he was just trying to get things organized so that he could figure out what needed doing. He might be the resident manager and general Mr. Fix-it, but that didn't mean he knew how to do everything. But he did have a well-used set of do-it-yourself books. First, though, he had to see what needed fixing.

"I'm just checking out the apartment, making a list of what needs to be done."

Her eyes moved to his hands, and her mouth turned downward. "A list?"

"A mental list."

"You'd better have a good memory."

She mumbled the last as she turned and almost stomped into the bedroom with her dress. He heard the closet door slide open, and he shifted his position so that he was able to see her put the hanger into the closet. That done, she took a good, long look around the room itself. He could almost hear her thoughts as the expressions flitted across her face. First, she gazed lovingly at what appeared to be an antique quilt on her bed. He'd lived in the islands long enough to know that a quilt like that would be worth a great deal. He'd never seen such an old one, though, and he expected it was some kind of family heirloom. The tenderness in her expression as she looked at it, smoothing out a wrinkle he couldn't see, confirmed it.

Once she'd determined that the quilt was okay, her expression turned to one of deep distrust. Carefully, she scrutinized the articles lying on top of her dresser, then studied the rest of the piece of furniture as though examining it for purchase.

He, however, knew exactly what she was doing.

"I'm not a thief." His mouth in a tight line, he slouched in the doorway, one shoulder pressed into the wood of the frame. There was no temptation to smile this time. He was *not* amused by her suspicions.

Momi didn't smile either. She merely continued her mental inventory. After another minute of careful inspection, she shot a fulminating look at him before moving back into the living room. She did not comment on his statement.

For the first time in three years, Rick debated his decision to keep the details of his life private. He found this woman fascinating—definitely a complication in a new lifestyle meant to be uncomplicated. As a successful businessman—in a previous existence—and as the owner of the apartment building, he felt sure he would automatically command her respect. She wouldn't be checking her lingerie drawers to see if he'd been peeking into them if she knew he owned the building.

Rick's mouth was pulled so tightly, his lips thinned to the point of nonexistence. Getting her to accept him as he was now—that was the challenge. And he'd always loved a challenge. He'd find a way to become friends with this proper librarian—and without sharing his secrets.

Chapter Three

"**W**as it really necessary to make this mess?"

Back in the living room, Momi gestured toward the stack of furniture near the kitchenette. "You've effectively blocked off the kitchen, which is an important part of the apartment. Especially if the bathroom sink is still out of commission," she added, moving toward the kitchen counter, where more of her possessions were stacked. She had hoped that Rick would contradict her about the state of her bathroom plumbing, but nothing was forthcoming.

"And if you ruined any of my decorations, I'll expect you to replace them or reimburse me for them," she added, her gaze settling on an unidentifiable pile of colorful miscellany on the counter. Her Halloween decorations—pumpkins, ghosts, witches, bats, and spiders—had been arranged around the two rooms in a cheerful manner. Now they were heaped on the counter like so much trash.

Rick shrugged. He couldn't believe the amount of Halloween junk she had strewn around the place. "I needed to see how much of the carpet was wet and try to dry it out."

"Not doing too well, are we?"

Rick just watched her. She had a very expressive face. A very pretty face. Such a shame she was obviously thinking that she'd like to hit him over the head with the nearest blunt object.

"I was checking the carpeting when you came in, seeing how it was seamed when it was installed. It does go throughout the apartment," he added, his eyes glancing meaningfully toward the bedroom, which did indeed contain the same off-white Berber continuing from the main room. "I want to lift it up on some blocks—it will help it dry faster."

"Faster would be good," she admitted.

He almost smiled as she avoided an apology for her earlier thoughts. True, she had not voiced them, but they both knew what she'd been thinking—or suspecting—about his time in her bedroom. She did, however, lower her eyes in a manner he read as embarrassment; it was almost as good as an apology.

"Will it help with the smell?"

Rick sniffed but said nothing. He knew what she meant, but he had an insane desire to make their time together last as long as possible. And he sure did enjoy seeing her eyes spark with anger. Besides, as soon as she got close to him, all he could detect, odor-wise, was the sweet, floral scent that surrounded her.

"It smells like a dirty pond in here," she added when he didn't respond.

"It's just the damp. That's what happens when things get soaked through."

He saw unhappiness flood her eyes.

"Isn't there anything we can do?"

Rick's heart melted. No sarcasm in her voice this time, just a heartfelt plea. He suspected that this was the real Momi at last. She seemed like a sweet, competent person. He was sure part of her frustration came from not being able to handle the situation herself. He knew she worked as a children's librarian, so undoubtedly she was used to taking charge.

"The place just needs to dry out. Unfortunately, the weather isn't cooperating. A few hot, sunny days would dry it right up." He shrugged. "I'd offer you another apartment, but we're full up."

Her gaze moved to the wide front windows, the ones that looked out across the central courtyard. Heavy raindrops continued to fall. The sky remained gray; it seemed to hold enough rain to continue for the rest of the day. Momi sighed. She looked close to tears, and he fought the protective instinct that made him want to take her into his arms and reassure her that everything would be all right. He longed to comfort her with a hug and a kiss, but that would probably earn him a slap across the face. He could do without that, and it would *not* be a step toward friendship. His best bet was to get that faucet fixed ASAP. He didn't expect her to fall into his arms with gratitude, but it should at least predispose her to liking him.

"These apartments are old, of course," he said. "Things like plumbing only last so many years."

"Yes, I know," she said. "I did look at newer places, even some condos. But this location is perfect. I love being near the ocean, and it's convenient for work too."

Momi continued to be distracted. She should find out Rick's last name. Perhaps calling him Mr. Whatever would put them on a more formal, businesslike basis. Create some distance between them.

He wore a shirt this morning, but there was still something very masculine and appealing about him. Momi couldn't quite define what it was. The wide breadth of his shoulders? The muscular frame she'd noted the night before? The long, strong legs, visible beneath his shorts— deeply tanned and sparsely covered with golden hair?

He smelled of clean male, with an undertone of some exotic spice—just the way he'd smelled last night, fresh from his shower. Was it his aftershave? Shampoo? It was so much more subtle than the miasma of cologne that had surrounded many of the men at Jade's party last night. And it was a lot better than the mildew smell from her sopping carpet.

"It is a great location. And among the last of the rental apartments in this area. All the others have been converted to condos. I've been refurbishing each unit, usually when they're vacant between tenants. But you wanted to move in right away, so there wasn't time to do more than paint and clean the carpet." He looked around the disheveled room. "But now, well, it might be your turn."

"My turn."

Momi couldn't help it. She had to laugh.

Rick turned toward Momi. After all her frowning and glares, he was surprised to hear her laughter. Worried at first that she had succumbed to hysteria, he soon realized that she was truly laughing. Such a musical sound, her laughter, one that seemed to infiltrate his bloodstream and hum through his veins. He smiled, then began to laugh as well. Her delight was infectious.

"Definitely your turn," he repeated.

What an attractive package Momi Kanahele was. Dangerously so. Rick found himself interested, and he wasn't sure he was happy about it. These last three years he'd done nothing but bum around the beach, fish, and take care of the apartments and the people in them. He'd made some casual friends, knew almost everything that went on in his units, but he'd kept his distance. The carefree existence of a carefree bachelor. It was what he wanted. Wasn't it?

Up until today—or perhaps last night—it had been.

The laughter wound down, and Momi looked over at him. "So, are you ready to start on the faucet?" She wiped a tear from the corner of her right eye.

Momi's question brought him out of his thoughts. "Not yet. But I'm working on it."

"Working on it?"

He could see what she wanted to do; he had to admire her self-control. He knew she wanted to yell at him, tell him to get it done now. But she was attempting to be polite, not wanting to antagonize him, probably. Staying on good terms with the help.

The grin that had been twitching at the corners of his lips turned into a frown.

"I need to have another look. See if I can just fix the cold-water tap or if I have to replace the entire fixture." He headed toward the bathroom and peered beneath the sink. "Also, I'll have to check to see if there's damage to the wall. And determine if the carpet can be salvaged."

Momi accepted all this without comment. But she trailed behind him as he walked toward the bathroom, her eyes on the faded Aloha shirt he wore. It was a disgraceful piece of clothing, the kind of shirt a wife would toss into the trash and the husband would snatch back out. If he didn't smell so good, she'd think it—and he—was dirty. But it must just be old and stained. Still, she scolded herself, it wouldn't do to wear something good for fixing the plumbing. She hoped that meant he was prepared to begin work on her faucet.

While Rick went to the hardware store, Momi spent her time pressing towels into her carpet, attempting to take some of the water out before he lifted it to dry. He'd told her that once he got back, he would lift the carpet from the floor and place some kind of blocks under it so that the air could circulate around it and speed the drying process. He assured her it would work and hopefully help with the musty odor.

She also reorganized her things. With no water in the bathroom, she had to have access to the kitchen. What had Rick been thinking, blocking access that way? Or didn't he think at all?

As she packed the Halloween things into a box, she examined them carefully, glad to find they had survived Rick's heavy hand. She'd take them down to the storage room and bring up her Thanksgiving decorations.

She was returning from the lower-level laundry room with a basketful of newly dry towels when she met Rick heading for the stairs. He held a toolbox in one hand and a couple of plastic shopping bags in the other.

"I hope that's a new faucet for me," she said, her eyes on the shopping bags.

"Right here," he said, holding up a bag.

She could see the glint of stainless steel inside, and she smiled. "Wonderful. It will be great to have things fixed. I've been working on the carpet, and it's feeling less soppy."

He grinned, that devastating grin that seemed to smack her right in the solar plexus. His eyes positively danced when he unleashed that grin and flashed his dimple. So she averted her eyes, suddenly finding it necessary to watch where she placed her feet.

Still, she could hear the amusement in his voice as he spoke from distressingly close behind her.

"'Soppy,' huh? Is that a word?"

"Sure, it is. I just used it, didn't I? That's how new words are brought into the language—from people using them."

Momi started for the stairs, but before she could put her foot on the first riser, Rick stopped her.

"Don't you want to know what's in the other bag?"

His voice had a teasing quality to it different from the sarcastic or the flirting tone he used so often.

Momi looked over his face, pausing as usual at his eyes, noting the fun in them.

"I assumed it held more plumbing supplies."

"Well, you'd be assuming wrong," he told her.

Another grin almost made her drop the basket of towels and leap into his arms. How could he be so darn attractive when he didn't do a thing to enhance his appearance? She'd always hated the grunge look, preferring men who took pride in their appearance. Was it that indifference to public opinion that made him so appealing?

"I got a gift for you." His grin widened.

"A gift?"

Momi smiled in delight—before she warned herself to be more leery and sobered her expression. "What is it?"

Her eyebrows drew together as she gazed at him with suspicion.

"Just a little something. I saw it at the store and thought you deserved a gift for all you've put up with."

She couldn't help it. Her smile broke through again. She loved surprises.

Rick offered her one of the shopping bags. No fancy wrapping for him. Momi suspected that, even if he'd had the time, she would have received the gift in its plastic bag with the store logo on it.

She set the laundry basket on the floor and took the bag. Whatever was inside had been wrapped in tissue paper, so she got to unwrap it after all.

"A candle?"

Momi lifted a thick pumpkin-colored candle from the plastic bag. A whiff of clove drifted to her nostrils.

"A scented candle." Her wide smile was genuine. She loved scented candles. And this one had a holiday-themed perfume—two of her passions melded into one: candles and holidays.

"I thought it might help with the smell."

Momi scrunched her nose at the thought of the musty aroma in her apartment. "One can only hope."

She raised the candle to her nose, sniffing delicately. "It smells like a pumpkin pie."

"Yeah. I hope you like pumpkin pie."

"My favorite."

She didn't say so, but it also smelled somewhat like Rick. She didn't know if it was his soap or his shampoo—obviously it wasn't aftershave, as it looked as if he didn't. Shave, that is.

She took another deep breath. "It's wonderful," she said. Though she didn't know if she'd be able to handle burning it. Every breath would bring Rick to mind—not only because he'd given it to her but because it shared that special clovelike scent that seemed to hover around him. It would also remind her of his strange appeal.

Then again, she was a big girl. She could handle it. And she had the quilt. Any day now her true love would arrive and banish all thoughts of Rick-the-apartment-manager from her mind.

"*Mahalo*." She placed the bag carefully into the laundry basket, beside the towels, then picked the whole thing back up. "It was very nice of you to think of that."

Together they climbed the stairs toward Momi's apartment. On the landing, she balanced the laundry basket on one hip so she could reach for the door. She didn't see that, from her other side, Rick reached around to open it for her. It was a kindly gesture, but the heat of his arm so close to her body, actually brushing lightly against her upper arm, caused so potent a reaction in her, she lost her hold on the basket and sent her clean towels tumbling down onto the floor and upper steps. The lovely candle hit the cement with a loud crack.

"Oh!"

Still gasping from the confusion brought about by her unprecedented reaction, Momi fumbled for the falling basket. Rick reached for it too, and their heads almost collided above it. Instead, they both stopped, almost cheek to cheek, each with one hand on the plastic laundry basket.

Momi's breath stopped in her throat, causing a lump that refused to move. Her eyes met Rick's startling green ones, something close to fear in hers meeting the amusement in his.

He thought this was funny? She was dying from an onslaught of strange and unsettling emotions, and he thought it was funny? He wasn't smiling, but she could see one corner of his mouth twitching, as though he was holding in his laughter.

Momi grabbed on to her anger once more. It was safer by far than trying to decide what was happening to her whenever he was near.

"I've got it," she said, pulling the basket from his grasp.

Rick let go immediately—so quickly, in fact, that Momi almost fell backward down the steps. She rocked perilously for a second before his hand shot out, his palm pushing into the small of her back, allowing her to catch her balance and right herself.

She took in a breath but still felt oxygen deprived. She'd need more than one quick breath to get over the feel of his hand on her lower back. She suspected that his handprint was scorched into her skin. She could still feel the heat of it.

"Go on in and get started," she said. "I'll just pick up these towels."

But Rick was already leaning down, gathering up towels and stacking them in the basket. Lastly, he reached for the bag holding the candle. Momi watched him part the tissue to examine it. She heard again the *crack* as it hit the floor and wondered if her wonderful gift was now so much trash.

"It's okay," he said, placing the package carefully beside the towels.

"*Mahalo*," she murmured once again.

She mumbled it reluctantly, though she knew he deserved thanks. He didn't have to help her; she'd upended the basket all on her own, because of silly romantic notions that had no place in their relationship. So it looked as if she would continue to be in his debt.

Afraid she'd been acting rudely, Momi turned toward Rick, ready to apologize and escort him inside—only to find that he was no longer there. Looking around, baffled that he had moved so silently, she noticed a pair of large rubber slippers beside her door.

Leaving hers beside them, she entered the apartment. He must already be in the bathroom, getting the job done, she thought. She'd find another way to thank him later. Maybe with some pastries she could pick up when she went shopping. Guys always liked pastries, didn't they?

It took Rick some time to remove the old faucet and set in the new one. He didn't have a lot of experience with plumbing work, though he was eager to learn. At least Momi didn't hang over him, watching his every move. He could hear her moving around the apartment, and that was distracting enough. He didn't know if he would have been able to work with her standing beside him in the tiny bathroom. Her reaction to his gift had been touching, and he pictured her finding a place for the candle as she puttered around the apartment. She looked in occasionally to gauge his progress but said little.

When he was done, he called her in, smiling proudly as he showed off the results of his handiwork. The chrome of the new faucet shone brightly in the clear lights of the small room.

Momi smiled happily. "It looks great."

"Go on, try it out," he urged.

Momi reached for the faucet, turning the cold-water handle to the on position. Nothing happened. Her eyebrows drew together, creating tiny wrinkles above her nose. She turned her gaze toward Rick.

Feeling embarrassed, Rick gave a quick laugh that had little to do with humor. Damn, but he was being a fool about this woman. She was beautiful, but he'd met lots of beautiful women since he'd moved to Kona. Lots of beautiful women in bikinis, in fact. So why did this particular woman in her jeans and T-shirt get under his skin?

But there was no denying the special chemistry that crackled between them whenever they got close. He'd almost felt singed there on the landing when he'd reached around her to open the door. And then again when he'd touched her back to help her regain her balance. It was the reason he'd escaped so quickly inside while she was still grappling with her own reactions. Because he *knew* she was experiencing the same thing.

"Guess I forgot to turn the water back on," he said, trying to add a chuckle that came out sounding strangled.

Ducking beneath the sink, he reached for the valve that would open the pipe and let the water back through. He turned the valve until it stopped, then stood again. He brushed his hands against the fabric of his shorts.

"There you go. Try it now."

His smile of pleasure that he'd fixed it himself turned to a grimace of horror as Momi jumped back and screamed. A plume of water flew toward the ceiling, drenching them both and everything in the room. The brand-new fixture remained in place but leaning precariously to one side. Water blew out all around it.

Biting back the words that wanted to pour from his mouth, Rick hurried back underneath the sink, turning the valve as fast as he could. No matter how quickly he turned the water back off, he knew it couldn't be soon enough. Momi was sputtering in outrage, her hair and clothes dripping. She looked worse than she had the night before.

She sputtered a series of wordless sounds before managing to say anything comprehensible. "You should have called a real plumber—it's clear you haven't any idea how to fix something like this."

Rick sat on the floor, not sure what to say. He deserved

her scorn, and he knew it. It wasn't that he'd wanted to save money by doing it himself. He just liked the feeling of accomplishment he got when he repaired something with his own hands. It was some kind of primal urge, he supposed, that desire to do something useful with your hands.

In addition, he was mesmerized by the sight of Momi. She might be wet, bedraggled, and infuriated, but the sight of her left his mouth dry. He didn't know if he could speak, if he would even know what to say.

Momi had the figure of a woman back when women were represented by Marilyn Monroe, not some stick fig-ure who weighed all of sixty pounds. Her hair dripped, curling wildly around her face and down her neck and back. Knowing how most women felt about frizzy hair, he thought she might be upset about the appearance of it, but he thought it the sexiest hairdo he'd ever seen. She'd had it that way briefly the night before—before he pre-sented her with the lilies and she'd gathered it up on top of her head. He had noticed that the native dancers seemed to prefer that wild, frizzed look. Did Momi?

But Momi was not looking at her reflection. Her eyes were blazing. By all rights, he should already be dry from the heat coming his way.

"I demand to know how to reach the landlord." She was sputtering, drops of water flying off her drenched hair.

He couldn't help it. His mouth began to turn upward into a smile. She looked so cute. So funny.

The smile turned into laughter.

Stunned, Momi stared at him. How dare he laugh at her? He had a lot of nerve. Besides, she wasn't the only one who was wet.

Rick's faded old Aloha shirt clung to him much like her own did. For someone she suspected was a beach bum, he looked darn good.

But then, what was she thinking? Of course he looked good. He probably spent all his time surfing, swimming, and working out.

Disgusted with her thoughts as well as with the person she thought he might be, she turned away—bringing her face-to-face with her reflection in the mirror. Her eyes widened as she surveyed her wet self.

Her clothes were completely soaked, her jeans a much darker blue than they'd been five minutes ago. And her hair! It had already been on the frizzy side from the dampness of the rainy day. Now the wet strands frizzed and curled and flew everywhere. Long, thin spirals twisted down her neck and over her shoulders. She'd actually put on a bit of makeup earlier, experimenting for a hoped-for date with one of her new acquaintances. And now the mascara she'd applied so carefully was running down her cheeks, like mime makeup gone awry. She looked ridiculous.

Momi found she couldn't help it either. Her lips tipped upward.

Her gaze found Rick's. Together they laughed at the silly situation. Okay, he might be incompetent, but he was just the building manager, after all. He couldn't know everything about fixing things; he was probably just an all-purpose handyman. He'd made a good effort at drying out her carpet, even though he'd wrecked what little organization she'd managed to impose on the limited space.

Somehow she brought herself under control and flicked her hair back from her face. With all this dampness, it would be a hopeless mess. She'd just have to pull it all into a ponytail. But not now.

She turned toward the door. "I'd better go change."

"You don't have to do that on my account." Still sitting on the floor below the sink, he raised and lowered his eyebrows in a creditable leer. "Personally, I'm enjoying the view."

"You're sick, you know?" But she couldn't hold back a chuckle.

"I've been called worse."

He grinned like a mischievous child who knew he'd be forgiven anything because he was so cute.

His words trailed after her as she rushed out the bathroom door, her cheeks stained with rising red. What was she thinking? Where had that come from—that comparison of Rick to a small, mischievous child? A child too cute for words? Rick wasn't cute. He wasn't ugly either, but he wasn't cute. He was . . .

Her mind slowed as her feet squished through the carpeting that led from the bathroom to the bedroom. The carpet that had been feeling somewhat drier was now soaked again. The carpeting in the bedroom door-way felt damp too.

How could she be wasting so much time trying to find a word that described Rick's looks? He was just a guy. He wasn't handsome or ugly, just an average-looking guy. Well, an average-looking guy with fasci-nating eyes and a devastating grin.

Okay, so he had potential. He had a mature, manly look but the clothes and posture of a teenage boy.

With a deep sigh, Momi closed the bedroom door be-hind her and pulled off her wet clothes. She had used up her change drying the towels. She might have to cart everything over to her parents' house and use their dryer.

Her eyes looked from the wet clothes she was bundling to the old red and white quilt. It was beautiful, the leaves and flowers twining across the fabric, defined by exquis-itely tiny stitches. If she did go over to use her mother's clothes dryer, she might be able to learn more about how Great-great-grandmother Helen's quilt worked.

From the bathroom, Rick watched Momi until she closed the door behind her, then pushed himself off the floor. With a sigh of his own, he leaned over the sink, examining the broken tap, wondering just what he'd done wrong. He was sure he'd done everything the way his books instructed.

He'd have to get a plumber now, he thought, looking at the new fixture and the space that had opened up around it. He'd used the tape, just the way the instructions said.

Maybe he hadn't tightened it enough. He glowered at the wrench and pliers still lying on the counter. Maybe he didn't have the proper tools. So much for that sense of accomplishment that came from working with his hands. In this case, all he'd achieved was an acute sense of frustration.

He was still scowling when he heard Momi's bedroom door open, and she appeared in the doorway.

"Have you figured out what happened?"

"Yeah. I was a fool to think I could do it myself."

He saw Momi's eyes soften.

"Well, I'm sure you were trying to save the owner a little money—and that's certainly commendable. But sometimes it's better to just go with an expert. It can even save money in the long run."

Rick felt more than foolish. She was making excuses for him, trying to assign an altruistic motive to his actions, when all he'd meant to do was entertain himself by working with his hands and ogling her superb figure. Now he not only felt like a fool but like a first-class jerk as well.

"I'll call a plumber right away," he promised. He gathered up his tools, tossing everything helter-skelter into his toolbox. "I'm sorry to delay things for you this way. I was sure I'd be able to fix it. It won't be too much longer."

With an abrupt nod to Momi, he left the apartment.

Chapter Four

"So, how's the apartment?"

After her difficult day, Momi was glad to hear Jade's voice on the phone. A quick glance at the clock made her realize it had been a mere eight hours since she'd left Jade's house that morning, not the days it seemed.

"The apartment is still a mess," she said with a sigh. "Even worse than before. I can't believe it. And the smell! It's like a rank pond."

"Better be careful—it might be mold."

Momi groaned. Just what she needed—something else to worry about.

"There's been a lot more information on molds in recent years. Some of them are deadly, but any mold can create allergy problems."

"Could mold develop that fast?"

"Sure. It's not my area of expertise, of course, but we did study molds in some of my early biology classes. I'm sure you don't have to worry about killer mold, but you don't want any kind of mold growing in your apartment. You should ask to have the carpet and pad replaced before it gets any worse. Is the management seeing to having things fixed?"

Momi couldn't help it. She laughed. "I guess. Such as it is. This isn't one of those high-class apartment complexes with a lot of staff. Nothing like the condos at The Orchid House," she said, mentioning the resort complex where Momi and Adam lived. "The thing is, I love this place because of its location and homey atmosphere. But the manager—who lives right below me, by the way—is it as far as maintenance staff. He seems okay but maybe not too bright."

As she said it, Momi recalled some of her conversations with Rick and realized that this assumption of hers might not be correct. Rick had an extensive vocabulary. Every now and again he used a word that jarred her just because it seemed out of place coming from his mouth. There was obviously more to him than met the eye.

"He looks like a beach bum," Momi continued, "and what I've seen of him since I moved in supports that. He rarely shaves, wears old, worn clothing, and seems to spend most of his time on the beach."

"But he did fix your faucet."

"Yes and no." Momi remembered that fiasco quite

well. She was still unhappy about it, though not as angry as she'd been when it happened. In fact, in hindsight, it was actually rather humorous.

She explained the situation to Jade.

"So you still have no water in the bathroom?" Jade's voice rose at the end of the sentence. Momi could tell she was incredulous. In just over a year of marriage, she had obviously gotten used to the kind of comfort and care offered by the Orchid House.

"Only at the sink," Momi hastened to tell her. "The tub and shower and the toilet all work just fine. And he lifted the carpet so that the air could circulate around it, and it's drying fairly well. It makes it interesting getting between the bathroom and the bedroom, but I'm not complaining, because it's working. It sure would help if it would stop raining, though."

Outside the open window, she could clearly hear the rain as it dripped off the roof onto the vegetation below. She could no longer hear the raindrops striking the roof, so she hoped the weather system was moving on.

"Meanwhile, I'm trying to relax and think happy thoughts. You know, so that the *mana* in Great-great-grandmother Helen's quilt will work. It seems like it would help if I could relax, don't you think?"

"It couldn't hurt," Jade replied.

"You don't sound like you believe it would help."

She heard Jade sigh.

"I was just remembering that when I first met Adam, there was a lot going on, a lot of stress. I was just starting a new job, the hotel was being sold, and we were all afraid about what that would mean for the research center. I *was* happy—about starting my dream job, about having my own place, and about getting the quilt from Mom. But there was a lot more going on."

"Okay." Momi laughed, a short sound without much humor in it. "I get it. I should just go on with my life and not stop everything, waiting for the quilt to work its magic."

Jade laughed, but hers was filled with amusement. "That's about it. So maybe you were right after all. You need to relax."

This time they laughed together.

"I guess I am a bit anxious."

The laughter had ended, but Momi could imagine the smile that her statement caused on the other end of the line.

"I wouldn't be surprised," her sister answered. "So, go ahead with your plan. Try to relax. Go on thinking happy thoughts. Someone will come along. And—who knows?—it might be someone you meet at work, like I did. Or someone at the supermarket. You may have already met him and not know it. That's how it was with me, remember?"

"I'll try to relax," Momi promised. "But it's going to be hard with my plumbing still a mess. And the carpet is all soaked and smelly." She heaved a heavy sigh.

"Come stay with us until it's all taken care of," Jade urged. "We have plenty of room."

Momi was tempted and told her sister so. "But I won't. I got this place because it's so convenient for me. You're too far from the library, and I wouldn't relish the long drive. Besides, I've been enjoying the fact that this place is all mine. It's the first time I've been able to afford an apartment without a roommate."

"I can understand," Jade said. "But the offer stands. Let me know if you change your mind."

"I will."

"And, Momi, about the quilt . . ."

Jade's voice sounded hesitant as she continued. "I used to have dreams," she admitted.

"Dreams?"

"Yes. Whenever I'd pull the quilt up over me during the night. At first I didn't remember what they were about—I'd just know that I'd been dreaming. Later, I realized I was dreaming about Adam."

"Wow." This was a whole other area that Momi hadn't heard about. Her mother certainly hadn't said anything about dreams when they'd spoken that afternoon. "I've been very careful with it," she said thoughtfully, "because it's so old and fragile looking. So I haven't used it as a cover. I usually fold it to one side when I turn down the bed."

"I know. I worried about that too. I used to fold it at the bottom of the bed, but then I'd pull it up during the night, without even realizing it." She paused. "But, the thing is, if you do meet someone, you can try sleeping under the quilt."

Now Momi was curious. "What were your dreams like?"

"I kept dreaming about swimming with wild dolphins," Jade told her.

"Of course." Momi smiled.

"It was a troublesome dream," Jade insisted. "It would start out nice and peaceful, then the water would begin to churn, and I'd feel like I was drowning. It wasn't until Adam showed up, swimming with me, that the dream turned beautiful and comforting again. I'm sure it was Grandmother Helen speaking to me."

"Wow." Momi was aware she'd said the same thing just a moment before, but it was the only comment that came to mind. This new knowledge about the quilt brought a new excitement—something she needed after her trying day. "I hope Grandmother Helen will visit my dreams too."

"Good luck."

Before Jade could say any more about her experience with the heirloom quilt, Momi heard a male voice at Jade's end.

Jade made hasty apologies and said she'd have to go. "Adam and I have a late dinner date," she said, before wishing Momi a good night.

Momi hung up with a smile. She couldn't wait to meet her true love. She wanted what Jade had with Adam—married over a year and still girlishly giggly about going out to dinner with her husband.

She'd barely hung up when the phone rang again.

This time her younger sister was on the line, bursting with curiosity about the previous night's party and whether the quilt had had any effect on Momi's life yet.

"I want to keep up to date for when it's my turn," Ruby told Momi. "I can't wait to finish school and get a real job and have my turn with the Lovell quilt. Sometimes I don't know what possessed me, going to school for so long." She ended with a heavy sigh.

Momi laughed. "Don't be silly. You've always been crazy about animals. Becoming a vet is the perfect career for you. You'll be done with school before you know it."

There was another heavy sigh. Momi suspected that Ruby was having a tough week. Perhaps she'd only gotten a B on a test, instead of her usual A-plus.

"I guess you're right," Ruby conceded. "So . . . I really called to check up on the quilt. Have you met anyone yet?"

Momi chuckled. It made her feel positively old to hear Ruby's enthusiasm, even though she herself had accepted the quilt with a great deal of eagerness.

"Remember, I haven't had the quilt for long. And so far nothing significant has happened. I did meet some nice guys at Jade's party. I didn't lack for dancing partners, or for companions just to talk to or have a drink with. A few asked for my phone number."

"So, do you think one of them was the one?"

Ruby's voice was still so full of excitement, Momi hated to tell her she didn't know. But she didn't.

"Well, I was expecting bells to ring and stars to

sparkle, maybe even an aura of rainbows when I met him. I figured, if the *mana* in Grandmother Helen's quilt is powerful enough to bring true love, there should be some indication of its happening."

She heaved a heavy sigh. She was still disappointed that Jade had killed that expectation. She'd looked forward to such romantic thrills.

"But there was nothing. Not even a few sparks. I talked to Jade a little while ago, and it doesn't sound like she heard bells ringing or anything when she first met Adam."

"I don't think she liked him much when they first met," Ruby agreed.

"I don't know about that," Momi said, "but she definitely didn't get stars and rainbows. It's a shame too. I would have liked to hear bells ringing."

"Who wouldn't?" Ruby paused for a moment. "Maybe it's just as well. I have so much more schooling, it's no use my worrying about how long it takes you to meet someone. Mom said the quilt is always passed along when the woman finishes her education."

"Yes, though I got it a few months after graduation, because Jade wanted to wait for my birthday. Mom also said it would work quickly, but I'm thinking that that can change too. Things might be different for me."

Unless one of the men she'd met at Jade's party was destined to be her true love, then the quilt still hadn't brought anyone special into her life. She'd just have to wait and see. Jade had met Adam the day after she received the quilt, so things were definitely different this time around. Her mother had said she met their father on her first day at work, but she hadn't specified how long that was after she'd received the quilt.

"I always believed in the quilt, even when Jade was telling me it was all a lot of superstitious nonsense and I should know better." She had to smile, recalling the conversations she'd had with her sister back when Jade had first come into possession of the family heirloom.

None of the sisters had known about the special quilt until after Jade received it upon completing her education. Their mother had presented it to Jade the weekend before she started working full-time for Dolphin Life Research at the Orchid House Resort.

Jade admitted to skepticism about the story her mother told about the "Lovell women's legacy." It seemed that in the early part of the twentieth century, their great-great-grandmother had fashioned the quilt during a difficult pregnancy. The story told of the great love she poured into the project—her *mana,* her soul. Because she never quite recovered from her daughter's birth, dying before the child's first birthday, the *mana* was especially powerful. She called her quilt *Ka Makani Ka`ili Aloha,* "the wind that wafts love from one to another."

Her husband, Thomas, had treasured the special quilt, dreaming of his beloved Helen on many nights as he slept beneath it. Then, as his daughter approached her eighteenth birthday, Helen came to him via a dream, instructing him to give the quilt to their daughter upon her graduation from high school.

Thomas had complied with his late wife's wishes, never thinking to question what some might have called an apparition or a mere dream. Dreams were an important part of Hawaiian culture. Ancestors often came to their descendants in dreams; they could also manifest as earthly objects—animals, plants, or minerals. In these incarnations, they were called *'aumakua,* and they looked after their descendants and could also be approached when guidance was needed. The Kanahele family *'aumakua* was a dolphin. Momi's older sister swore that a dolphin had saved her life when she'd wandered too far from shore at the age of six. Momi had never doubted it. That experience had shaped Jade's life, leading her to become a marine biologist and work toward educating the public about the preservation and care of dolphins.

Jade had not, at first, believed in the story of the quilt—that the *mana* wrapped within it was powerful enough to bring the women in the family their one true love. Like the scientist she was, she'd called it "ridiculous" and "superstitious nonsense." Yet she'd been unable to ignore the special chemistry that flowed between herself and a resort guest who happened to be the son of a well-known developer visiting the hotel with an eye to purchase.

Momi, however, had always loved the romantic story of the quilt. She couldn't wait until it was her turn.

She'd pestered her mother and grandmother for whatever they could remember, not only about Helen's story but about their own experiences with the quilt. There had never been a divorce among the women directly descended from Helen Lovell, and all their marriages were solid and loving. The quilt was a great legacy, one Momi hoped would not be ruined by her experience with it.

Still, she'd had the quilt for barely a week. There was lots of time for it to work its magic.

The two sisters went on to discuss Jade's party and Momi's plumbing difficulties. As they said their good-byes, Ruby reminded her older sister to stay in touch.

"I expect you to keep me informed, okay? About the quilt and who you meet. And when."

Momi assured her that she would.

It wasn't until they hung up that Momi recalled Ruby's words about Jade and Adam. "I don't think she liked him much when they first met," she'd said. Momi felt a chill seep into her spine. She'd recently met someone she didn't like. Heaven forbid.

Besides, she and Jade had talked about how she and Adam had met, and Jade had never said she didn't like him at first. Just that she didn't think he would be the one the quilt brought. But she didn't even believe in the quilt at that point.

Jade did mention that tingling feeling she used to get that told her Adam was nearby. It sounded like a very special chemistry. It was all so romantic. Nothing at all like her situation with Rick. There was some chemistry there, she had to admit, even if she couldn't explain how it could exist. Because she didn't like Rick. He was so irritating, and he didn't seem to care about anyone else or what others might think of him.

Of course, he had given her that scented candle, and that was a very nice thing to do. And he'd helped her with her costume the night before and even gotten the flowers for her.

But half the time he acted like a dirty old man. No, while he might be older, he wasn't quite old enough for that appellation—so that made him merely a jerk or a cad.

Brought to a standstill by her conflicting thoughts, Momi decided to make it an early night. She was tired after being up so late the night before and from the work she'd done in the apartment that afternoon.

She entered her bedroom and stood still for a moment, just looking at the wonderful red and white quilt. Thoughts of Rick fled quickly as she thought of what Jade had said about her dreams. Would it be cool enough to sleep under the quilt tonight? There was a hint of a chill in the damp air. And once more she could hear raindrops pinging off the roof.

Momi sighed. The rain might mean she could use the quilt and see what dreams it brought, but it did not bode well for drying out her apartment's carpet. Or for getting rid of the musty, moldy smell.

She looked toward her dresser top, where the

pumpkin-pie candle burned. She couldn't tell if the candle helped with the odor or if she had just gotten used to it and no longer noticed. But every now and then she caught a whiff of clove. The scent brought thoughts of Rick and a faint flutter in her midsection.

Momi carefully folded down the old quilt. She sure hoped that little flicker was indigestion caused by the peanut butter sandwich she'd eaten for dinner.

Momi stood in the doorway of a large dining room, with a beautiful table set for a feast. Perhaps Thanksgiving dinner. The chairs were all filled, but she couldn't quite make out the faces of the people sitting in them. There were both adults and children—she was sure of that.

Then she walked toward the table, carrying a platter with a lovely roasted turkey. The turkey was browned to perfection, stuffing spilling out of its cavities. Vegetables carved into fantastic flowers surrounded it. She carried the platter to the table and put it down in front of the man sitting in the place of honor. She couldn't tell who it was, but she was certain it was not her father. Because she also knew that she loved that person unreservedly, and with a romantic love, not a filial one.

Momi strained to get past the blurriness of the vision but could not. She began to feel frantic, trying so hard to see yet unable to. Her heart beat so fast, she could hardly breathe, but still, she could not see. . . .

Momi sat up in bed, feeling flushed, her forehead

beaded with sweat. Her heart still beat too rapidly, and the sense of frustration held as she recalled every detail of her troubling dream. The beautiful table set for a feast—a table and a room she didn't recognize. People she loved—she was sure of that. Yet she wasn't able to make out any of the faces. It was very odd.

As she brushed hair out of her face with slightly unsteady fingers, she looked down at the old quilt. She'd slept under it, as Jade had suggested. And just as her sister said, she'd had a dream. But the dream hadn't told her anything, just left her feeling frustrated.

Well, it showed her hosting a big Thanksgiving dinner, carrying in a beautifully cooked turkey. That was interesting. Because Momi didn't cook. She was notorious in her family for her lack of interest in cooking. A couple of years ago she'd interned at a library in Honolulu, and her roommate had decided to teach her to cook. Momi made an attempt to learn—her roommate had been so eager to help her out that she hadn't the heart to tell her she just wasn't interested.

But the experience merely reinforced her conviction that cooking held no appeal for her. You spent hours working on a meal, and in less than an hour the whole thing was gone, devoured by the friends you'd invited in to try it. Momi had learned to cook a few things—she could do a nice spaghetti and meatballs dinner (with bottled sauce), and she was a whiz at pancakes from scratch. But for the most part she still wasn't interested.

She'd much rather buy frozen dinners or patronize the deli at KTA.

So what did the dream mean? Did Grandmother Helen expect her to learn how to cook? Jade said her dreams were about swimming. As a marine biologist, the ocean was definitely Jade's milieu. A dinner table was not Momi's. Though it seemed to be a holiday dinner, and Momi did love the holidays.

Momi threw back the covers and climbed out of bed. She couldn't worry about it now; she had to get ready for work. The dream had been interesting, but it just brought more frustration. No sparks, no bells ringing . . . and now no clear meaning to what appeared to be a special dream. She was sure her ancestor was trying to tell her something. She just didn't know what it was.

Chapter Five

Momi welcomed the busy day at the library. It left her with little time to think, and after the past two days, she appreciated that. With her dream fresh in her mind, she spent her lunch hour poring through the cookbook section, wondering if Great-great-grandmother Helen had been trying to tell her she had to learn how to cook if she ever wanted to meet her true love. Her mother had been hinting at the same thing for years, but it was harder to ignore someone who could haunt your dreams.

Returning home from work, she had a déjà vu encounter on the staircase. Just as on the previous day, she had her arms full when she met Rick going up to her place. Today it wasn't a laundry basket but an overflowing armful of thick, heavy cookbooks.

Momi had one foot on the first step, heading up to her apartment, when Rick's voice stopped her.

"Ms. Kanahele." Rick nodded graciously.

She took a deep, steadying breath. She tried to tell herself that it was her anger at the man—at his attitude and incompetence—that made her heart race and sent tingles up the back of her neck. Yet she was afraid that the truth of it was—she hated even to think it!—he was just too physically appealing. Who could have guessed she, Momi Kanahele, would be so attracted to a beach bum? If there was one thing she'd always admired in a man, it was ambition. And success. And good grooming. And now, just as she was hoping to meet her true love and start a new life, she found herself grappling with the potent chemistry between herself and this least ambitious of men.

Suddenly she remembered what Jade had told her about tingles on the back of her neck. Shock and horror had her denying any association between Jade's experience and her own. There was no way this man could be her true love! Why, she didn't even like him. It was just chemistry, the way some women were attracted to entertainers and movie stars. Her Grandma Lucas still had a crush on Elvis, and he'd been dead longer than Momi had been alive.

Momi completed her step up before returning Rick's nod, arranging what she hoped was a polite smile on her lips. She liked the advantage in height she enjoyed by being on the first riser. Rick was a tall man, but that one step brought them nose to nose. She could look directly into his phenomenal eyes. . . .

Perhaps it wasn't such a good move after all.

"Mr. . . . uh . . ." She stopped as she realized that she didn't know the man's last name. He called her by hers quite a bit, but all he'd ever given her was the name Rick. "What is your name, anyway?"

"It's Rick. Rick is fine."

Momi frowned.

"Sure, Rick is fine. If you're calling me Momi. But when you call me Ms. Kanahele, I feel strange calling you Rick. It's a little too *Upstairs, Downstairs,* you know?"

He stared at her for a moment, and she thought he wasn't going to reply. Perhaps he didn't understand the television show reference. The series was an old one, and she'd never seen it, but she did know about it and its theme.

"It's Mahoney," he finally said. "Rick Mahoney. But, please, call me Rick."

"Okay, Mr. Mahoney. I'll call you Rick as long as you call me Momi."

"It's a deal."

Too late it occurred to her that holding to "Mr. Mahoney" might have put some distance between them and helped her keep him there. Was it a mistake to insist on first names?

"Let me help you with some of this stuff," Rick said.

He reached for the books, his hands passing beneath hers to take the bundle. Chills raced up her arms at the touch of those warm hands against her arms.

"What is all this anyway? Do librarians have homework?"

Disturbed at her involuntary reaction to his touch, Momi frowned, trying to pull away. "I'm fine. I have them."

"Don't be silly." His voice was determined. "Come on, come on. You don't have to be that tough. I know you're a strong, independent woman. Just let me help you out, okay?"

Pressing his point, his hands pushed farther beneath the bundle she carried. She could feel the hair on his arms brush against the inside of her wrists. The sensation sent a new wave of chills racing through her system.

Reacting on gut instinct, Momi pulled away from his warm hands and their ability to make her tremble—and the books tumbled over their arms and onto the floor. Déjà vu.

Momi sighed even as she dropped down to pick them up. Rick, however, did the same, and their heads came within a millimeter of slamming into one another. Again. So close, in fact, she could feel his breath on her cheek. The chill that shot through her arms a moment ago faded into nothingness as her entire body trembled. She came close to landing flat on her `ōkole, recovering herself just before she ended up sitting on the cold cement.

Rick caught the quick movement that signaled Momi's save. He was sure she'd almost landed on the floor, and he thought he knew why. His breath had fanned across her cheek, and he was close enough to detect the shiver that ran through her. That reaction of hers produced a quick intake of breath on his side—bringing with it a lungful of her special scent. Her elusive scent tantalized him. It was something floral and tropical, but he'd yet to determine just what. It had been driving him nuts.

Much as he hated to, he needed to put some distance between them. She smelled so good, and Rick enjoyed pleasant stimuli. It was a shame to deny himself but totally necessary.

With an inward sigh, he grabbed up as many of the oversized books as he could and stood. What on earth was she doing with all these?

Momi quickly picked up the few remaining volumes and got to her feet.

"What is this?" Rick asked. "The entire *Encyclopedia Britannica*?"

He glanced down at the books now loaded into his arms. They were almost all thick, many of them oversized. Right on top was *The Joy of Cooking*. He cocked his head to check out a few more spines. *The Martha Stewart Living Cookbook. The Everyday Turkey Cook-*

book. *Happy in the Kitchen. Dream Dinners*. They were *all* cookbooks.

"Cookbooks, huh?" He gave her an assessing look. "Planning a party?"

She'd lived above him since July, and very little noise came from her place. Her work schedule varied. When he did hear voices up there, they were all female. He didn't recall her ever having what he'd call a party.

Momi blushed. Now *that* was interesting.

"Ah. Cooking dinner for a man, I bet." Rick was surprised at the disappointment that came with that thought. He wondered if she'd met someone at that party she was so hot to attend on Halloween.

"No!"

Her response was so quick, Rick believed her. And felt immediately better.

There was something there, though, lurking behind those chocolate eyes. Was it embarrassment?

He grinned. "Don't tell me. You don't know how to cook?"

Momi sighed, and a world of frustration was in that brief sound. He could see her mind working through her options. Admit she couldn't do something most women were expected to be expert at? Lie? His grin widened.

Momi turned and trotted up the steps.

Rick followed her, his lips twitching into a real smile. So the librarian had a shortcoming. Not only that, but trailing at just the right distance behind her, his arms full of her books, he got to admire the view as she climbed upward. *And* the shapely legs beneath the skirt that ended just above her knees.

When she reached her door, she stopped. She'd probably just realized she didn't have her key ready to open the door, Rick thought. And now she was stuck out there, with him expecting an answer.

He imagined she counted to ten, because it took a full ten seconds before she turned to face him.

"Okay. I don't cook. I admit it. In fact, I'm a disaster in the kitchen. I've just never been interested in cooking. But I had this dream last night where I was hosting a wonderful dinner, and I thought it might mean that I should finally learn."

Rick looked into her earnest face and knew she was telling him the truth. She really believed her dream had sent her a message.

"You don't sound too enthused." He balanced the tall stack of books he carried on the corner of the railing and reached for her purse, which she'd laid on top of the books she carried.

"What are you *doing*?"

Rick chuckled. "Is that all you can ever think of to say to me?"

While she was still looking outraged, he found her key, opened the door, and gestured her inside.

At least she seemed relieved to deposit the books she held on to the counter. Though she also cringed when she looked at the carpet still propped up to dry and fairly well blocking the entrance to the bathroom.

"You could have asked me for the key."

"So you could be outraged at such forward behavior?" Rick shrugged. "It was easier—and faster—to just take it upon myself to find it and let us in."

He put his load of books down next to hers. "I knew you wanted to unload those books," he added, nodding toward the stack she'd so quickly set down.

He shoved her purse into her now empty arms. "You might want to check this, in case I stole something while I was searching for your keys."

He was satisfied with her flush of embarrassment.

"I trust you," she told him. A bit lamely, he thought. But he'd had his fun. He was willing to change the subject.

"So, why aren't you interested in cooking? Don't you like to eat?"

He made himself comfortable, leaning against the counter, his legs crossed at the ankles.

"Of course I like to eat, but it's not the center of my day. Cooking is a lot of work, and in no time at all the food is gone, and you have to start all over again."

Although she'd professed to trust him, he noticed that she checked her purse as she spoke, fumbling with both her keys and checkbook before snapping it shut and putting it on the counter.

"I'd rather do crafts or read," she said. "Or just about anything else, I guess."

"Cooking is easy." He sounded a bit smug and hoped she didn't notice. But after his unsuccessful attempts at fixing her plumbing, he felt proud to admit that there was something he could do and do well.

"You cook?"

"Don't sound so incredulous. Cooking isn't hard. You just have to know how to read and how to follow directions."

"So you taught yourself?"

"I did. Learned from the Internet, actually."

"And is what you cook edible?"

Her eyebrows rose with the question, and she tilted her head in a most alluring manner.

"Momi, you wound me!" He put one hand against his heart, as though she'd just shot an arrow through his chest.

Why did she find it so hard to believe he could cook? Maybe it was because guys weren't supposed to cook? But then, looking at it that way, women were supposed to. And she didn't.

"I'll believe you're a great cook when you invite me over for something wonderful," she said.

Rick stared at her for a moment. In the three years he'd been managing the apartment, he'd tried to keep his distance from the tenants. He valued his privacy and didn't want them to know that he was more than the manager. But Momi had been insinuating herself into his consciousness ever since she moved in. They may not have actually met until two days previously, but he'd been fully aware of her since the day he showed her the empty apartment.

"Tell you what. I'll teach you. I make a great meat loaf. I'll come over tomorrow and show you how to make it. What do you think?"

"Meat loaf?" Momi sounded uncertain.

"What, are you a vegetarian?"

"No. I guess meat loaf would be okay."

Rick watched Momi's face as she thought over his suggestion. He didn't realize why his simple recommendation merited so much thought, but he could see her debating something with herself. The tip of her tongue ran across her lips as she thought. Then the edges of pearly white teeth bit lightly into the fullness of her lower lip as she continued to work out whatever it was that bothered her.

Wondering what was so difficult, Rick admired the way she poked her tongue out to think. It was the kind of thing he often saw young children do as they played on the beach, when they needed to concentrate on a difficult task. Definitely cute.

Maybe she didn't like meat loaf. But why didn't she just say so? So far in their brief acquaintance, she had not been shy about speaking her mind.

Finally her face softened, and a friendly smile widened her lips. Rick knew she'd reached a decision.

"Can you roast a chicken?"

He was so surprised, he stared at her for a moment before answering. Then he blinked. "You want to roast a chicken?"

Momi nodded eagerly. "I'd like to learn to do that.

Thanksgiving is coming, you know, and someday I might have to do a turkey. But I think it would be better to start with something smaller."

He nodded. "Okay."

Happiness blossomed, transforming her from pretty to beautiful. Rick was mesmerized. The librarian was full of surprises. He'd like to hear more about that dream of hers. But he'd have to wait to approach that; he knew she'd clam up if he asked about it now. He wondered if it had something to do with Thanksgiving dinner.

"When do you want to get together?" He glanced toward her small kitchen. "We'll have to see what supplies you need." He eyed her speculatively. "You have to make a shopping list before you can cook a dinner."

Momi clucked her tongue at him. "I know that. I'm not a complete idiot."

"Good." He finally pushed himself off her counter, straightening to his full six feet.

"I called a plumber."

That certainly got her attention. She stared at him, eyes intent.

"He couldn't come today, but assured me he'd be here tomorrow to take care of your sink."

"Great. Thank you."

She nodded solemnly at him. She was polite, he had to give her that.

"Have you talked to the landlord about the flood damage?" she asked.

"Ah . . ."

"You know, the carpet and pad? Except for my costume, that's the only thing that was damaged." Momi frowned at him. "It wasn't my fault that the faucet broke, so he's responsible for the damages. And the smell is part of that. I'm afraid it's from the damp, and there's a real danger of mold. He should replace the carpet and pad. That's probably the only thing that will help."

Rick watched her. Should he tell her that *he* was the landlord? In his years of ownership, he'd kept his true identity a secret. He liked being regarded as a regular guy—and he liked working with his hands. Painting, tiling, all the handyman things he'd never attempted when he'd been an upscale professional man on the mainland. His ex-wife would never believe that he found such pursuits fulfilling. She'd have been horrified if he'd tried to fix their plumbing.

"It's all taken care of," Rick finally said. There was no reason to explain the details. He'd decided to tear out the carpet in Momi's apartment and install tile instead. He was good at tile; he'd practiced in his own apartment. And the maintenance on his part, as well as the tenant's, was much easier. Now he just had to inform her, let her know he'd get started as soon as the tiles were purchased.

He should have known it wouldn't be that easy. As soon as he informed Momi about the tile flooring, she was all over him.

"Tile? Instead of carpet? Do we have to? I like carpet. It's so nice on bare feet."

"Tile is nice too," Rick told her. "It's cool in summer—very practical here in the islands. Easier to keep clean too. You just have to dust and mop it, or sweep up the sand when it gets trailed in. You don't even need a vacuum cleaner, just those cleaning pads they sell nowadays."

Momi still didn't look convinced.

"I have tile in my apartment, and it's great. The carpet and pad in here got so wet, you're right about mold being a possibility. Mildew can be a problem so close to the ocean anyway—even without a flood." He glanced toward the window and back. "But at least the sun is shining again."

Momi nodded as he listed the advantages of having a tile floor. "Hmm."

"What does 'hmm' mean?"

He could tell she was still thinking it over.

"You make a good case for it," she finally said, shrugging in acquiescence. "I guess the landlord has decided, so it doesn't matter what I think anyway, yeah?"

"Yeah." Rick thought it interesting the way the islanders often ended a sentence with "yeah" in the way he himself might use "huh." He'd even found himself doing it recently.

"And you say you're going to go pick it out?"

Uh-oh. He might have given her too much information. He nodded. "Uh, yeah."

"Good. I want to go with you."

She looked ready to grab her purse and leave immediately.

"You don't have to do that," Rick said.

"I know. But I'd like to help."

Rick started to feel a touch of panic. It had been years since he'd felt anything similar, but he recalled the sensation, and it wasn't pleasant.

"There isn't much choice involved. Just plain white tiles like the ones in the kitchen and bath. You can put all your furniture in those rooms while I work."

Momi frowned. He didn't blame her; it was going to be another huge imposition.

"What about the bedroom?" she asked.

"I guess we could leave the carpet in there, if you'd like. It didn't get soaked, so it will probably be okay. I can cut it off at the threshold."

"Good. I'd like that."

She looked around the apartment as though visualizing its future appearance.

"You have done this before, right?" Her brow furrowed as she questioned him.

Now he was starting to feel offended, and she apparently recognized that emotion in his expression.

"No offense, Rick, but you aren't exactly great shakes in the plumbing department. You did try, but it didn't work out too well. And I haven't seen any other examples of your handiwork."

"Okay, so I haven't done much plumbing. I'll have

you know, though, that I did the tile floor in my apartment and in units five and seven. I would have done this one while it was empty, except the carpet looked good, and you wanted to move in right away."

"Okay." She nodded, as if satisfied with his qualifications. "But I'd still like to help. I like to learn new stuff, and I love doing crafts. Home improvement is a lot like craft projects, you know. This could be really helpful when I get my own place. You can show me how it's done, and I'll help you."

Rick's eyebrows rose in surprise. He hadn't expected her to make such an offer.

"I don't know. I'll have to check about insurance . . . and stuff."

It sounded lame even to his ears, but he wasn't sure he wanted to be working around Momi. She could be more than distracting.

"I'll let you know. I'd like to get it done before Thanksgiving."

"No problem," she said, tossing a saucy grin his way. "Especially if I help out."

Chapter Six

A pounding noise, like *pahu* drums playing for a particularly unrhythmic hula, woke Momi from a sound sleep. She'd been dreaming again, too, once more about food. What was it with Grandmother Helen and food?

Throwing back the covers, noting that she had indeed been sleeping beneath the heirloom quilt, Momi stumbled toward her front door. She did have the presence of mind to stop and look through the peephole, however.

Rick. She groaned but bowed to the inevitable and opened the door.

"What is it? And did you have to tell me about it this early?"

She glanced back into the apartment, brushing hair out of her face as she tried to focus on the clock. Her hands rubbed up and down her arms, which showed the raised bumps of chicken skin. "What time is it, any-way?"

Rick had heard her groan before she opened the door. He knew it meant she'd looked through the peep-hole and seen him. Now *he* wanted to groan. It wasn't that early—almost 9:30. But she was delightfully sleep bedraggled, her eyelids slightly puffy, her hair flowing in all directions. She was absolutely gorgeous. He wanted to forget about their shopping trip and cooking lesson and just take her into his arms and spend the rest of the day in the gloomy apartment. He'd take care of those goose bumps in no time at all.

With effort, he pulled his mind from that direction. He couldn't go there. Besides his personal rule that he did not get involved with any of the tenants, she wasn't his type. He liked a more carefree kind of woman. Momi was rather intense.

"It's almost ten," he said, stepping inside. A little ex-aggeration never hurt anybody, and it might get her eyes open faster. The quicker she lost those half-closed bed-room eyes, the better for him. "You just need some light in here," he added, stepping to her window and opening the blinds.

Momi blinked as the the Kona sunlight suddenly streamed into the room, brightened even more when he strode into the kitchen and opened those blinds as well. She frowned, staring at the clock as if she might see a different, earlier time. He just knew she'd like to yell at him for getting her up so early—except that it wasn't so early. Also, along with the light came fresh, outdoor air. As it was warmer, it would soon disperse the cooler night air still trapped in the rooms.

The apartment now bright and cheerful, he had to admit she'd done a good job with her decorating. Even with his aversion to holidays, he found her fall décor in honor of Thanksgiving appealing. There were colored leaves spread around arrays of fat candles on both the dining and coffee tables. There was a squat pumpkin on the counter and a happy-looking turkey on an end table—way too happy for its being so close to Turkey Day.

Having run out of things to look at, Rick found his eyes turning inevitably back to Momi in her silky pajamas. As he glanced over her for a second time, he saw her eyes narrow, her eyebrows almost meeting above the bridge of her nose. He grinned. He was in for it now.

"*What* are you staring at?" she almost shouted. "Can't you show any manners? You should turn your back until I can go in and change."

"Hey, you opened the door. You should have changed before you did that if you don't want to be seen in your pj's." His grin widened. "I don't know why you're so shy. The view is terrific."

Momi blushed scarlet, rushing into the bedroom and slamming the door.

"Good thing your downstairs neighbor isn't in," Rick called after her.

Momi leaned against the closed bedroom door, her hands on her burning cheeks. *How* could she have opened the door for Rick, wearing her rayon pajamas? She liked the feel of the silky fabric, but it clung to her body in an embarrassing way. If she hadn't been so disoriented from being tugged out of that dream, she would have had the good sense to pull on a robe. Then perhaps he wouldn't have looked at her as if she were the main course at the Thanksgiving feast.

Blinking in remembrance, she realized that the dream had once again been about a Thanksgiving feast. The abrupt awakening from Rick's door pounding had interrupted it, but she recalled being at the same dinner table she'd seen in the first dream. Once again, she'd brought in the turkey. She was leaning over, placing it before the man at the head of the table, when she woke up. She'd hoped to see the face of the man this time. Even though she didn't remember all the details of the dream, she did recall that leaning forward filled her with love and anticipation. What else could have been meant? She was sure she was supposed to see who it was—would have seen him, if not for Rick's early wake-up call.

She pushed herself off the door, suddenly desperate to get into the bathroom but knowing she couldn't go out there again until she'd put on her street clothes.

She pulled her pajamas off as quickly as possible,

stuffing them into a drawer without bothering to fold them, as she usually did. Just as quickly, she donned underwear, a long-sleeved T-shirt, and jeans. Then, suitably attired, she dashed from bedroom to bath.

By the time she reentered the living room, Rick had made himself at home in her apartment. She could smell coffee, and he was taking bread out of the toaster. As she approached the dining table from one end of the room, he approached from the other.

"You don't have much in your kitchen. This was the best I could do for breakfast." He put the plate he carried in front of her—surprising her. She'd thought he was feeding himself.

Momi looked down at the plate, which held two slices of toast. Already on the table were a plastic container of spreadable margarine, a jar of her mother's guava jam, and a butter knife. While she stared at this display, Rick returned to the kitchen, returning almost immediately with two mugs of coffee.

"At least you have some good coffee," he said, setting the mugs down, one in front of each of them. "Do you need sugar or milk for yours?"

Still stunned at his display of homeyness, Momi barely heard him. "You made this for me?"

No one except her mother had ever made her breakfast, even something as simple as this. College students rarely bothered with more than coffee or soda and Poptarts or a granola bar, so none of her roommates had done so either.

Rick made an elaborate show of checking the room. "You see anybody else in here?"

Impulsively, she bounded around the table. Throwing her arms around him, she stood on tiptoe to place a kiss on his cheek.

"*Mahalo,* Rick."

Her voice came out soft and raspy, like his cheek. The stubble he always wore produced an interesting tingle in her lips and an almost irresistible urge to further explore the sensation.

As though scorched, Momi released him, almost jumping back in her hurry, and scurried around the table to her chair.

Rick cleared his throat. "Do you want milk or sweetener before I sit down?" he asked her again.

His voice sounded almost as rough as his cheek had felt. Momi swallowed before answering. Something was lodged in her throat, but clearing it would have told him way too much. She hoped he couldn't hear the way her heart was pounding in her chest. Bounding around the table that way was just too much exercise for so early in the morning, that was all.

She concentrated on breathing normally as she reached for the jar of jam. "No, thanks."

In lieu of clearing her throat of its tightness, she swallowed again. "This is so sweet," she added. "Not the jam, though that's sweet too, of course. I mean your fixing me something to eat while I changed."

Darn, she was babbling. She took a bite, chewed, and

swallowed before offering a gentle smile. "You're not as mean as you try to make out."

Rick frowned at her as she bit into the toast. "Don't go seeing what isn't there. I was looking through your kitchen to see what we'd need to buy—for the cooking lesson." His arm swung out, indicating the kitchen area. "You don't have much of anything in there. Do you ever eat here?"

"Sure. All the time. But I eat at my parents' a lot. My mother *loves* to cook. And to pass out leftovers," she added with a smile.

"But none of that rubbed off?"

Momi shrugged. "There wasn't any reason to cook when I was at home and she was doing it. Then, while I was getting my degree, I was busy."

She took another bite and chewed. So she wouldn't have to say more. It wasn't up to him to tell her how she should have been living her life. She wondered when *he* started cooking.

She swallowed, took a sip of her coffee—he'd made it just the way she liked it—and decided to ask him.

"Just when did you learn to cook? From your mother?"

He smiled. "As a matter of fact, yes. She believed that everyone should learn to cook one or two basic items so that they wouldn't starve. She taught me to make meat loaf and spaghetti. After—"

Rick stopped abruptly, as though catching himself. Momi looked up, curious.

"I had more time *after* I moved here," he continued, placing a slight emphasis on the word *after*. "That's when I taught myself to make lasagna and rack of lamb, among other things."

"Rack of lamb?" Despite herself, Momi was impressed. She might aspire to cooking a perfect Thanksgiving turkey, but she'd never even attempt rack of lamb.

"I've always liked it. It seemed sensible to learn to cook things I like."

"Can't argue with that. Do you put the little fringe-y papers on it?"

He eyed her for a second before answering. That saucy grin could get addictive.

"No, I don't. And you're thinking of a crown roast of lamb—that's the one that uses the frills." When she raised her eyebrows in a silent question, he added, "the 'little fringe-y papers.'"

Momi finished off her toast and cupped her hands around her mug. "Thanks again. That was good." She took a sip of coffee. "So, did you make up a shopping list for us?"

"I did. But I think I'll have to add to it after seeing your kitchen. You don't even have basics like flour and butter."

Momi shrugged. "You don't need flour to heat up microwave dinners or stuff from the KTA deli. And I use margarine." She nodded toward the plastic bowl on the table.

Rick shook his head. "What am I going to do with you?"

Momi frowned. "Nothing. It's none of your business what I do inside my own apartment. But since you've offered to help me learn this stuff, I'll accept your verdict on the state of my kitchen. And your help in stocking it."

Rick almost laughed when she nodded at him, for all the world like a Hawaiian queen bestowing her grace on a subject.

"I've made a list of some things I think everyone should have." He took a folded piece of paper from his pocket and held it up. "Besides coffee, sugar, and salt."

He noticed her grimace. That was about all she had in the place, except for the stale bread he'd used for the toast and a jar of *umes* in the fridge. Despite his time in the islands, he had not acquired a taste for the red, pickled Japanese plums. He'd even checked the freezer, in case she kept her flour there, but it held nothing but frozen dinners and Häagen-Dazs.

"Come on," he said, getting up and taking his mug and her plate to the sink. "Time to get cracking."

By late afternoon, Momi was ready to retreat to her bedroom and slam the door, much as she had that morning. She'd called Rick "slave driver" more than once, but he kept at her. Still, she had a small chicken browning in the oven, and a pot of potatoes boiling on the stove. More than at any time since she'd moved in, the apartment felt like home. The cooking smells also helped disperse the last of the musty dampness that had bothered her since Halloween.

As she washed the dishes they'd used, Rick took time from his drying to look around the room. "What happened to all those cookbooks you had the other day?"

"I took them back. After you mentioned the Internet, I checked it out and decided I didn't need all those cookbooks. I can just look for recipes online and copy them out as I need them."

"Does that mean you've already done that?" But he shook his head and answered his own question. "No, you couldn't have. You didn't have enough supplies to make anything worthwhile. No eggs, barely any milk, no butter or cooking oil, no flour, a small box of sugar."

He looked over at her as if something had just occurred to him.

"Why did you have that, anyway, since you take your coffee black?"

"For friends who don't, of course."

The dishes done, Momi removed the rubber gloves Rick had suggested and laid them aside. She didn't know if she'd mention it to him, but that had been a thoughtful recommendation. Maybe she'd thank him later.

She opened the oven door and pulled out the rack, using one of her new mitten-style pot holders. The bird looked good and smelled heavenly. Rick had brought along a printed recipe, then shown her how to mix herbs and spices and rub down the chicken before putting it into the oven.

She took the turkey baster from the counter and suctioned up some of the drippings, releasing them back over the browning bird.

When she straightened up after closing the oven door, Rick was grinning at her.

"You're a good pupil."

Momi felt inordinately proud. She was also terribly tired.

"Let's go sit down for a while."

"You still have to mash the potatoes," Rick protested.

"I need a rest." Her stubborn tone made him raise his eyebrows, but he took a can of juice from the refrigerator and followed her into the living room.

"Tell me again why you're doing this," Momi said. She crossed her ankles, resting them on the coffee table. Her head fell back against the top of the overstuffed couch. "Gosh, I'm tired."

Rick smirked. "You don't get enough exercise. We haven't done anything today." He raised the tab on the juice can and took a long sip. "Probably too much partying last night."

Momi almost sneered at him. "I worked last night, and you know it. I saw you peering out your window when I came in from the library." She slouched down farther into the soft pillows, and her eyes lit up. "I did a special evening story hour last night. It was my first one, and it was a big success. There were twenty-eight children there for the Good Night Story Hour, lots of them in their pajamas and holding teddy bears. I can't wait to do it again."

Rick loved watching her when she got that glow on her face. It was obvious that she adored her work. *He* sure couldn't get excited about the thought of reading a story to twenty-eight little kids.

"The library director is letting me try lots of new things. He says I have such enthusiasm, I'm almost like one of the kids myself." She sighed happily. "Do you like to get all involved in your work?" she asked, startling Rick out of his thoughts.

"Me?"

Laughing, Momi made the same exaggerated looking-around movement he'd used that morning on her. "I don't see anyone else, do you?"

Rick frowned, though he could feel his lips twitch with the grin that wanted to burst out. He'd spent the past three years being careful *not* to get overly involved with his work. He'd spent too many years being engrossed in business matters, and he didn't plan to repeat the mistake. But he couldn't explain that to Momi without going into a lot of things he had no intention of sharing.

"Not really," he said, being careful to keep his voice deliberately casual. "You know how it is. Keep things simple, have fun."

Rick could see Momi gathering her thoughts for some kind of deep, philosophical discussion. So he finished his drink, pushed himself off the sofa, and held out a hand to help her up.

"Come on, up you go. Time to mash the potatoes and put on the green beans."

"Slave driver."

But she smiled when she said it.

Chapter Seven

Despite his hesitations and his qualifications about times and delivery dates, Rick had Momi's tile bought and delivered by her next day off. He'd tried to dissuade her from helping, but she'd set her mind to it. Momi even set her alarm for what was an unusually early hour for her—six-thirty in the morning—and was ready with coffee and her special pancakes when Rick arrived.

"You cooked?" Rick couldn't hide his surprise, but he grinned happily as he sat down to eat. "These look terrific."

Momi smiled, proud to present her best meal—up until her roast chicken, of course.

"I told you I was a whiz at pancakes. A roommate taught me. It's one of the few things I've enjoyed making." She bit into one of the fluffy disks, chewing and swallowing in pleasure. "Did you know you can buy

100

these little shape things to pour the batter into and make the pancakes come out looking like animals and things?"

Rick smiled at her. "Yeah, I did know that."

"I'm going to do that someday, when I have kids."

Yeah, Rick could totally see that. She'd get all excited about it too, just as she did about her Good Night Story Hour. She'd make a great mother.

And he was not the least bit interested in motherhood and family or any of that stuff, Rick told himself. If he'd spoken aloud, he would have used his firmest voice. As it was, he could only turn the subject of their conversation to a more amenable subject.

"I see you're ready for the DIY project." He nodded toward her work clothes. She wore faded jeans and the same old T-shirt she'd worn the day they were soaked in the bathroom.

"I'm looking forward to learning something new," she assured him.

Hours later, she was still smiling about her new skill.

"This is kind of fun," Momi told Rick as she carefully laid a tile over the mortar. "It's kind of like doing crafts. You feel so good about what you've accomplished." She sat back on her heels to admire her handiwork.

"That's how I feel about it," Rick admitted. "That's why I like laying tile. You can see what you've accomplished right away."

He, too, looked over their work so far. Almost half of the room was done.

"It's similar to cooking," he said, throwing a mischievous look her way. "You make something, you admire the way it looks and smells, and then you eat it."

Momi laughed. "Maybe. Unlike plumbing," she said, almost giggling as she added, "where you have to wait until you turn on the water and then the faucet to see what the results are."

Rick glared at her, but she wasn't offended. She could see the humor in his eyes. Boy, he did have the most amazing eyes. That wonderful color, and very expressive. For humor, anyway. She couldn't usually tell what he was thinking about otherwise, but she could always spot the laughter.

She'd been amazed at the amount of work they'd had to do before they could even start. She'd stored her things as best she could in the bedroom and kitchen, which had made cooking this morning rather interesting. She'd had to squeeze between the narrow space she'd left when she moved as many things as possible into the already-narrow room. In the bedroom, she'd carefully folded her quilt and stored it in the closet before pushing the bed against the wall and shoving the sofa and matching chair into the extra space. The dining table had to be left in the living room, but after breakfast Rick put it upside down on top of her bed.

Getting the floor ready had taken hours. Pulling up carpet was a lot harder than she'd envisioned. Then they'd had to clean the floor well before continuing.

"So, did you learn this stuff from your father?" She

put the spacers carefully into place before laying the next square of tile.

"No."

Momi frowned. His answer was so short and sweet, there was no wiggle room for her to inquire further into his background. But she could certainly try.

"So how did you learn to do this?"

"Trial and error," he said.

Inwardly, Momi sighed. It was too bad the man had no ambition, she thought. He probably would have made a great spy. He was closemouthed enough to have been a success at it.

"I was surprised that you start in the middle of the room," she said.

But even that comment didn't elicit any more conversation from the man.

Rick watched her from his peripheral vision as he continued to work. He knew what she was trying to do. She was curious about him and hoping to pry out information about his background. He'd been in the islands long enough to know how things worked. Hawaiians liked to delve into a person's history and family. On meeting someone, the last name was reviewed and mutual acquaintances and relations searched for. "What high school did you go to?" and "When did you graduate?" were two of the first questions that came up among locals meeting for the first time. Momi probably felt she wouldn't really know him unless she knew where he was from and who and what his parents were. Just the type of thing he'd moved here to avoid. Still, it was fun watching her try to achieve her goals. He wondered if she would try again.

He didn't have long to wait.

"Do you do other creative things?"

She was spreading the mortar now and concentrating on getting the ridges through it, so he felt all right about looking his fill. She was something to see, too, in a worn and faded T-shirt. Unfortunately, he'd had to warn her not to wear shorts, because of the wear and tear on the knees. But she'd surprised him by not only wearing an old pair of snugly fitting jeans, but producing a pair of knee pads she said were from her soccer-playing days in PE.

She knelt on the bare part of the floor, leaning directly over the tile she now set into place. But his favorite time for a peek was just after she set the tile into place, when she sat back on her bare heels and checked out her work. She did that after every piece she lay, still new enough at it to enjoy each successful placement. After every third or fourth tile, she would stretch her back, pulling her shoulders back as far as they would go, then rotating them to get out the kinks. He enjoyed watching her so much, it was slowing him down.

"Good grief," he said, as he watched her rise effortlessly to her feet from her previous squatting position on the floor. "How on earth did you do that?"

Momi laughed. "Years of hula lessons," she informed

him. "I'm great at duckwalking too," she said, demonstrating as she headed toward the kitchen.

He groaned, watching her smooth glide. He recalled the days when he'd had to duckwalk for some coach or other. His thigh muscles would hurt for days afterward.

Momi stood as she reached the kitchen, where she'd been careful to allow access to the refrigerator. "Would you like some water?"

He nodded. "Thanks." He stood, too, but not as gracefully as she had. "Probably a good idea to stretch a little before we continue."

Momi handed him a cold bottle of water.

"So, you mentioned coaches. What sports did you play?"

The woman was certainly determined. Still, he didn't suppose there was any reason not to share that particular part of his past. It was the more recent past he had problems with, the part just before he decided to chuck his lifestyle and relocate to Hawaii.

"I did the usual sports things. T-ball, Little League, Pop Warner."

He wondered if she would notice that the games he'd mentioned were all for young boys. By the time he'd reached middle school, he was more interested in computers than in sports. By high school, he was a fullfledged nerd. He'd even had the horn-rimmed glasses. He hadn't bothered with contacts until he'd reinvented himself at age twenty-nine.

"No soccer?"

"No. It wasn't as popular then, at least not with the boys. I knew a lot of girls who played."

Momi sat up at that and looked over at him. Their eyes met, and the air between them seemed charged with electricity. A spark or two would not have surprised him. In fact, a crackle from that invisible energy would not have been out of place either. But the whole thing was so unusual an occurrence, he instantly dismissed it from his mind.

"It wasn't as popular then?" she repeated. "When did you graduate?"

Rick blinked to break the eye contact and, with it, that strange pseudoconnection between them. He almost laughed at her question. He'd just been thinking of how important that question was among locals. He shouldn't be surprised that she'd asked. But he also knew that what she really wanted to know was, "How old are you?"

For one quick moment Rick thought he'd make her guess. But he filed that notion almost immediately, afraid of the ego blow she could deliver—if she thought him in his forties, for example. His hair was already going gray, though it was still thick. Happily, his many hours in the sun had bleached his light brown hair to a mixed gold, which made the gray harder to see.

Rick shrugged, using the motion to rock his shoulders back and forth. Bending over to lay tiles was not only hard on the knees.

"The popularity of sports varies a great deal from one part of the country to another."

Momi frowned. "I guess."

Rick wanted to laugh at the confusion that momentarily clouded her eyes. She was *really* curious about him now. He couldn't recall when he'd had so much fun.

"So, did you hear about Thanksgiving?" Ruby asked.

"Yeah, Auntie Clarice called," Momi said. She was lying on the sofa, children's books spread all around her as she vetted volumes for her next preschool story hour.

"It'll be strange not being with Mom and Dad and Jade, but I do love Auntie Clarice," Ruby said. "And the food will be great. She's expecting at least twenty-five people."

"Mom is sure excited about seeing the Caribbean," Momi said. Jade and her husband were going to spend Thanksgiving with Adam's father in the Virgin Islands and had invited the senior Kanaheles to accompany them, all expenses paid. They would stay at the luxurious Donovan Resort on Virgin Gorda, and Carol Kanahele was calling the trip a second honeymoon. "She says she always wanted to travel."

"Isn't it funny?" Ruby said. "You just don't think about your parents wanting to do things like that. A second honeymoon," she added with a giggle.

"Mom has a real romantic streak," Momi said. "It comes out when she talks about the quilt."

"Speaking of which," Ruby said, "tell me about the guys you met at Jade's. Did any of them call? And, more important, have you had a date?"

Momi drew in a deep breath. "Yes. I had two calls. Peter and Len."

"Two? Wow!"

Ruby's excitement carried across the line, but Momi was past that. She just wanted to tell her sister about the dates and move on.

"Peter is an accountant at the Orchid House. He invited me to a movie. It was very nice; we had a good time. But I don't think it will go anywhere. Sometimes you can just tell, you know?"

Ruby agreed.

"Then Len . . ." Momi paused. She didn't know how much of that disaster she wanted to share. "He's a real type-A personality. A lawyer. Let's just say it didn't go well. Our personalities clash."

"Details, I want details," Ruby whined.

But Momi remained firm. She wasn't sharing anything more. She didn't want to think about it. "Hey, I don't ask for details of your dates."

"Okay, okay." Ruby laughed.

Momi knew that her sister had a very active dating life at college; it was curious that she expressed such interest in the quilt and its powers when she seemed more than capable of finding her own true love.

"And you haven't met anyone else since you got the quilt?" Ruby asked.

"No. I haven't really had time, what with the plumbing disasters in the apartment and then the refurbishing work. The manager is a pretty decent guy, but he's not

real handy. His first attempt to fix the faucet was another disaster—remember, I told you about it. But he's
better at tiling. He's doing my whole place, replacing
the carpet with a very nice white ceramic tile, and it
looks good. He's showing me how to do it too. It's kind
of like doing crafts. It's a great feeling to look at the
floor and know I helped put that in."

For a moment Ruby didn't say anything.

"And had you met the manager before Jade gave you
the quilt?"

"No. I'd seen him around, but I didn't really meet him
until the night of the party when the faucet exploded."
Her disgust at this latter event carried clearly across the
miles.

"Aha! So there *is* another new man in your life,"
Ruby declared.

"Don't be ridiculous," Momi told her. But the thought
stopped her cold. "That's . . . that's impossible," she finally sputtered. "You might as well say the plumber
who was here to fix things is the one."

"Why not? Maybe he is."

Momi was stunned, even though she'd entertained
the same thought—very briefly. Rick as her true love?
Ruby didn't seem to understand what a horror she was
suggesting.

"Well, he just can't be," Momi said. "Not Rick and
not the plumber. I never even saw the plumber; he came
while I was at work. And Rick, well . . . He's . . . he's
old. And he's a beach bum."

"A beach bum? I thought you said he was the manager of your apartment building?"

"He is."

"He can't be a bum if he has a job, Momi." The logic of her statement was reflected in her tone. "Even if he does hang around the beach," she added. "Being an apartment manager is a lot of work. He's on call all the time, and people probably complain to him about all kinds of things. And he'd have to keep the place clean and all that stuff."

Momi couldn't refute Ruby's reasoning, but she wanted to explain to her the impossibility of Rick's being part of the quilt's mystique.

"You haven't seen him, Ruby. He's a nice enough person, but he dresses like a bum in old, faded clothes. He slouches, and he doesn't shave. He doesn't have a *real* job."

Ruby laughed. "I'll have you know that that unshaven look is really in right now and considered very sexy. Honestly, Momi, you've turned into a snob. Managing an apartment building *is* a real job. Maybe he's retired, or on disability or something. Some of the military guys fall in love with Hawaii and move here when they retire." She paused. "You said he's too old to be the one the quilt brought—how old is he, anyway?"

Momi thought for a moment, biting down on her lower lip in chagrin. "I'm not sure. He's older than me—I'm sure of that. He just seems old, you know?"

"Maybe he's just mature," Ruby suggested. "Hey,

I've got a great idea. Bring him to Auntie Clarice's for Thanksgiving. It'd be a nice gesture, and if you bring a date, the other aunties won't bug you about why you're still single."

Momi's mouth fell open at the suggestion, but then she began to consider it seriously. Now that she was done with school, the older relatives *would* be getting after her about settling down. If she attended the dinner alone, she'd have to spend most of the day making excuses for not having a ring on her third finger.

Why *not* ask Rick? She could tell him it was a thank-you for the cooking lessons.

"Maybe I'll do that," she told Ruby.

"Great. I've got to go—got a late class. I'll see you at Auntie Clarice's. I can't wait to meet Rick."

Momi gazed thoughtfully across the room after she ended the call. Ruby had certainly given her some things to consider. Oh, not that Rick could possibly be the man the quilt had found for her. That was too absurd to even mention. She'd dismissed that thought ages ago.

But the whole idea that he could be more than what he appeared, more than a beach bum. Okay, he did seem conscientious enough as apartment manager, even if he wasn't terribly handy. And to give him credit, he did *try* to fix her faucet right away. And he did a nice job with the tile flooring. It would be a lot easier to keep clean than the old carpeting too, just as he'd said.

But there might be more to his story. As Ruby had suggested, he could be retired military. Men retired early in the military, then had a pension to live on. An apartment manager's job might be just the thing for someone like that. And lots of military men fell in love with the islands during the time they were stationed there and then came back to live or to retire.

But Momi quickly dismissed that scenario. It was so easy for her to picture Rick. And when she did, he was slouching in place, hands in his pockets, or lounging in a doorway, or draped over her sofa. No, there was no way the man was retired career military. She knew men who'd been in the service, and their posture was a dead giveaway. You didn't spend twenty years in the military and then become a sloucher.

But Ruby's other suggestion . . . that he might be ill or handicapped or something. That was a possibility. Some disabilities were not obvious. Her brow furrowed in thought. He seemed healthy. But there really was no way to be sure.

She wasn't a snob—she was sure she wasn't. Lots of the children who used the library and attended her programs were poor. And she treated them and their families just as she would anyone else. Salaries were low in the islands, and everything was expensive.

Still, being an apartment manager was something she imagined people did as a moonlighting job, to get the free rent. Surely you didn't get health insurance with an apartment manager's job, or a retirement plan. And what about Social Security? She'd been raised to be practical, and to her a "real" job included all those perks.

On the other hand, he might have those things taken care of through some unknown factor, like a disability pension.

Momi got up and returned the phone to its cradle. She had a lot to think about. First of all, she had to stop jumping to conclusions about people. Look at how impressed she'd been with Len that first night. And he'd turned out to be a jerk of the first order. She shook her head.

Now, how could she get Rick to open up a bit more about himself? So far her attempts in that direction had resulted in failure.

A grin broke out when she remembered her second cooking lesson that weekend. That would be the perfect opportunity for her to try again. After all, she had learned a little about him while they were tiling—just enough to be *very* interested in learning more.

Their second cooking lesson was the first one Rick had so impetuously proposed that fateful day. He was showing Momi how to make his favorite meat loaf.

"So you really like meat loaf, huh?"

"What, you don't?"

Momi smiled, that quirky, mischievous grin that made his heart flip over.

"I'll let you know tonight."

She put the pan into the oven, set the timer, and turned back to him.

"You were right about cooking. You just have to follow directions."

He didn't think that needed a comment. He was more interested in the way her eyes were sizing him up. She was getting ready to pry again. Usually he would find some excuse to leave when a woman got that glow in her eye. But with Momi, he found himself looking forward to the challenge of keeping himself to himself. With a start, he realized that she was the first true friend he'd made since his move to Kona.

"You spend a lot of time at the beach," she said, running water into the dishpan. "My family used to camp out on the beach when we were young. I have some great memories."

Rick picked up a bowl, wiping beads of water from its smooth surface. Chicago had a lakeshore, but it wasn't conducive to camping.

He heard Momi sigh. His continued silence was getting to her.

"So, what did your family do for vacations? Did you spend lots of time at the beach?"

"Not really," Rick replied. He couldn't completely ignore her queries, but over the years he'd perfected the art of replying without divulging any real information.

Momi rinsed out the sink and removed her rubber gloves. Then she turned to him, hands on hips.

"Rick Mahoney, you are the most frustrating man! That meat loaf had better be out of this world."

And it was.

"This is excellent," Momi told him after her first bite.

"What I like about meat loaf is its simplicity and versatility," Rick said. "You can make it on a leisurely afternoon, like we did today. Or prepare the meat ahead of time and put it in the fridge till you're ready to cook it. And the leftovers are really good for snacks and sandwiches."

Momi nodded. "Good. I can make one of these and eat from it for a week."

Rick laughed. "You'll get tired of it quickly that way."

She shrugged.

"What shall we cook next?" he asked.

"I'm open to suggestion."

"Maybe this will help."

He'd escaped to his place after her short outburst earlier that afternoon, saying that he had to get some laundry done while the meat loaf cooked. But he did not spend all his time on laundry. After he'd put his clothes into the washer, he zipped out to the store. He still remembered Momi's delight in the candle he'd brought her and her revelation that she loved surprises. He wanted to see her smile at him that way again.

So when he arrived for dinner, he brought in a brown paper bag and secreted it beneath his chair. Despite her curiosity, he wouldn't let her peek inside.

Now he took the bag from its hiding spot and presented it to Momi. "Since you're so serious about learning to cook, I thought you should have someplace to keep your recipes. I got this for you."

Momi pushed her now empty plate aside and took

the bag from him. Her smile was all he'd hoped for. "I love surprises."

"I remember."

Momi delved into the bag, bringing out a white loose-leaf notebook. On the front, a creative font proclaimed it to hold *Momi's Recipes*. Inside she found a collection of plastic sheet protectors and copies of the recipes they had already prepared.

"And I included a few things I thought would be easy for you to do on your own. A good Crock-Pot soup, if you have one of those, and a nice marinade for chicken, among others."

"Rick, this is *so* nice. I don't know how to thank you."

Rick returned her smile. She didn't know it, but she'd already thanked him with her sweet smiles.

"No thanks necessary. It's nothing much. I just thought you should have a way to keep things together.

"It's wonderful," she insisted. Momi was so touched, she felt tears spring into her eyes.

Rick was such a mass of contradictions. One moment he was irritating her to the point of exasperation, and the next he could make her heart turn over with his kindness. And of course there were the times that her heart galloped from his slightest touch.

After putting the rest of the meat loaf into the refrigerator and the plates into the dishwasher, Momi led the way to the living room.

"Let's turn on the television. I think there's a Rainbow Wahine game on tonight."

Rick was amenable to watching women's college basketball. So, feeling relaxed after the nice meal and nicer surprise, Momi decided to broach the subject she'd avoided all day.

"So, what do you do on Thanksgiving? Do you make a turkey for yourself? Or . . . do you have relatives in town?" Momi didn't know why she'd never asked him that before.

"No relatives," he said. "I don't do anything special," he added, girding himself for the dinner invitation he could sense coming. Every year he had to field numerous well-meant invitations. Usually he remained holed up in his place, watching football, making a deliberately un-Thanksgiving-like dinner. Last year it was chili. "I'm not fond of holidays."

Momi waited, but he didn't elaborate. With a heavy sigh she finally asked him why. "Did something terrible happen one holiday?"

Her feet flew off the coffee table, landing on the floor as she sat straight up. A sudden thought made her heart turn over. "Oh, my gosh, you didn't lose your parents on Thanksgiving, or something horrible like that, did you?"

Rick laughed, but the sound had little fun in it. "Nothing like that, no. Still, I'd rather not talk about it."

Momi frowned. "Okay."

She settled back against the sofa, her eyes on the television even though she was barely paying attention to the game. She was more interested in talking to Rick—and watching him. Indirectly, of course.

"Well, why don't you come with me to my family dinner? Nobody should be alone on Thanksgiving, even if he doesn't like holidays."

It was Rick's turn to sigh. "If it's all the same to you, I'd rather not. I like staying home and watching football without interruptions."

Momi considered. Somewhere in the course of their brief acquaintance, she'd begun to like Rick. He tried to appear gruff and unemotional, but now and again she caught glimpses of another person entirely, and that was the person who intrigued her.

So she tried again. "Come on, I need a Thanksgiving date. Otherwise I'll spend the entire time explaining why I don't have one and fending off matchmaking mamas, aunties, and grandmas."

At his raised eyebrows, she explained about her parents being gone and how she and Ruby would be going to Hilo to their cousin's.

"She's my mother's first cousin, so she's really our second cousin, but because she's Mom's age, we've always called her Auntie Clarice. She's great fun— you'll like her. Ruby—that's my younger sister—said she's planning on around twenty-five people. The food will be fantastic," she added, hoping to tempt him that way.

"Younger sister, huh? This isn't the one who had the Halloween party?"

Momi was surprised he remembered that much about her family. But she supposed that she talked about them a lot. She had to, since he was so closemouthed about his own.

"No. I'm the middle daughter. That was Jade who had the party. Ruby is the youngest." She scrunched up her nose and added the explanation for their names before he could ask. People always did. "And, yes, we are all named for gemstones. My mother calls us her 'little jewels.'" Her nose wrinkled up in disgust.

Rick laughed. He thought it was cute. "So, what about Ruby?" he asked. "Is she taking a date for Thanksgiving dinner?"

Momi shrugged. "I don't know. But she's still in college, so it doesn't matter as much for her. But I'm done with my education, so they'll all be thinking it's time I settled down."

Rick looked into her face, trying to see inside her mind. His voice lowered to something just above a whisper. "And what about you? Do you think it's time to settle down?"

Her reply would do a lot to help him decide if he would go or not. He already felt much too comfortable in this woman's company. And he'd always thought she looked like the happily-ever-after type, a woman who wanted a walk down the aisle. He'd done that once and had not been happy with the aftermath.

Momi surprised him. "I want to have a family someday. I think I could even be ready for that, if I could find the right man. But finding the right person to share your life with is the most important thing. You can't just decide you want to settle down and someone instantly appears. No matter what the old aunties might want." Or what family legend claimed about heirloom quilts, she thought.

She shrugged. "I was hoping to meet someone special at that Halloween party. Remember?" Her eyebrows arched up, almost meeting her hair. "The one where my beautiful flapper dress got ruined?"

"How could I forget? You only remind me about it every other day or so."

"It was a very special dress," she said. Her voice sounded sulky even to her own ears, but it was hard not to resent the loss of that special dress for the party. She might have been successful with the *holokū* he found for her, but she had not met her true love. She couldn't help wondering if things would have been different if she'd worn her first costume choice.

"Hey, I had it cleaned for you, didn't I? Isn't it as good as new?"

"Yes, and I thanked you for that. But I can't very well use it for anything before next Halloween."

It had been very sweet of him to get her dress cleaned. And, much to her surprise, it did look as good as new. But Halloween was over and with it her one chance to meet someone special.

She almost sighed with frustration over the quilt. She'd had such high hopes, but so far, nothing. She'd dreamed again last night but was no wiser as to what her ancestor was trying to tell her.

Her eyes focused on the television screen, but her mind was back in her dreams. It was the same dream she'd had several times now. A long table was set for the Thanksgiving feast, and she carried in a perfectly roasted turkey. She knew now that she could cook well if she just set her mind to it and followed the directions in a recipe. But she still didn't know what the dream meant.

She sighed again.

Beside her, Rick found it impossible to concentrate on the game. Not with Momi sitting so near that he could feel the heat of her body. They weren't even touching, yet he was so aware of her presence, he could not focus on what was shaping up to be an exciting game.

He heard her heave another large sigh, and he began to feel guilty. She wanted his company on Thanksgiving, and he was making excuses. It wasn't her fault that he hated holidays because of what had happened to him on Christmas Eve three years ago. It was going to be her first year without her parents there too—a fact that was nothing short of amazing to him. He knew from papers she'd filled out to get her lease that she was twenty-four years old. How was it that in all that time she had never gone to a friend's for Thanksgiving? Especially to a boyfriend's?

Rick knew that family was important in Hawaii. `*Ohana,* they called it. It encompassed not only the immediate family but all the cousins, in-laws, and sometimes even old friends or neighbors that were *almost* like family. Still, the idea that she'd spent all those consecutive holidays with her family was daunting.

Despite his self-warnings, he discovered that he felt sorry for her. He'd caused her a lot of problems with her apartment, trying to fix the faucet himself and making even more of a mess, then disrupting her place for days while he ripped out the carpet and laid the tile. Accompanying her to a family meal to help her feel more comfortable seemed the least he could do.

Meanwhile, Momi was still trying to persuade him.

"I can guarantee a fantastic meal. Everyone contributes, and you won't believe the variety. 'Plenny good stuff,'" she added in local-speak, her tone wheedling.

Rick looked into her eyes and thought he caught a trace of vulnerability there. It was his undoing. She could be the tough, independent woman around him but maybe not around her family.

He sighed in turn, a big, dramatic heave of breath.

From his peripheral vision, he watched to see the effect this would have on his companion. The result was everything he could have desired.

She turned toward him, laying one dainty hand on his shoulder.

"Please? You won't have to make something to take—you'll be a guest. I'll make something for the potluck."

"You will?" He turned toward her, raising his eyebrows. "That's quite a sacrifice, coming from someone who calls cooking a waste of good time."

Momi shifted uncomfortably, her knee brushing his thigh for one brief, heady moment.

"You might be changing my mind about that," she admitted. "I've enjoyed our cooking lessons. Maybe the trick is to have good company?" She smiled sweetly at him as she said it.

He shook his head at her tactics. "Okay. I give in."

He looked directly into her eyes, lifting a warning finger for emphasis. "But no lies about our relationship. I don't want you telling anyone we're almost engaged or something."

Her bright smile shot straight to his heart, making it take a dip into his belly and back up again. Rick felt sixteen again, and he was really too old for that kind of emotional tumult. But he couldn't back out now, right after agreeing. Especially when she was smiling so happily at him.

"No problem. We're just friends. You're too old for me anyway, which I'm sure they'll be able to see. And you needed a place to eat on Thanksgiving. No one wants to leave a person all alone on Thanksgiving, so they'll understand why I asked you. I'm also sure no one will make a big deal out of my unmarried state if I have a man—even one who's just a friend—there with me."

She smiled happily at him, and for a moment he was afraid she was going to give him another of those impulsive hugs, maybe even another kiss on the cheek. Both were highly enjoyable—too much so. In this setting—so much more intimate than sitting at the dining table for breakfast—he wasn't sure he could trust himself to keep their relationship on its current friendly level.

"Thanks." She almost breathed the word, which floated across the space between them, soft and musical.

Rick swallowed.

He barely saw the rest of the game, though he remained seated on Momi's couch alongside her for the duration. He even made a few comments in response to hers. But mainly his mind was on her earlier words. He was too old for her? How did she figure that? He wasn't old. He knew that she was twenty-four. That didn't make her that much younger than his thirty-two. It was less than ten years, for goodness' sake. Plenty of men had wives more than ten years younger.

Not that he was looking for a wife.

When he got back to his own place later that night, Rick went straight to the bathroom to peer into the mirror. Momi's comment about age was *still* bothering him.

He did have lines in his face. Character lines, he liked to call them. Did they add years to his appearance? How old did Momi think he was? Men were supposed to look good as they aged, but that didn't mean he wanted to look like an old man.

He tipped his head, trying to get an angle that allowed him to see the top or back of his head. Was his hair thinning? His hairline might have migrated back a bit, but Momi couldn't know that. She hadn't known him when he was twenty-one, so she had no reference point for comparison. There was some gray, but it was barely noticeable because of the way the sun lightened streaks into his hair.

He turned from the mirror in disgust. Since when had he been so involved in appearances anyway? His indifference to such nonsense was the main reason he didn't let anyone know he was the owner of the apartment building. He liked his new career—if it could be called that—of apartment manager. He liked spending time on the beach, swimming every day, getting his hands dirty when work needed to be done. He'd had enough of the so-called good life to last him the rest of his life.

Chapter Eight

As he settled into bed on Thanksgiving night, Rick made the decision to avoid Momi in the future. After the day he'd just had, it was a matter of survival. If he wanted to maintain the carefree bachelor existence he'd enjoyed these past three years, he would have to stop seeing her.

Because he'd enjoyed Thanksgiving day.

They'd left Kona at dawn, driving to Hilo on the Saddle Road. Local lore said this road, which threaded between two of the island's mountains, was haunted, that marchers could be seen at night carrying their torches along the ancient trails. In fact, Momi had insisted they return via the longer, scenic route that followed the shoreline, even though it was too dark to appreciate the scenery. She didn't want to "disturb any spirits" on the Saddle Road after dark, she had told him.

The day had gone better than he'd hoped. Just as Momi promised, the food had been fantastic. He couldn't remember when he'd eaten so much, and even with all he'd taken in, everyone kept urging more on him. Momi's contribution was the prettiest platter of crudités he'd ever seen, and a huge success.

She'd found a Web site describing how to carve vegetables and fruits and decided it was as much fun as doing crafts. There was so much oohing and aahing over her radish and tomato roses, people had to be begged to eat them. She'd also made flowers and leaves from cucumbers, apples, and chili peppers.

"It's an ancient Thai craft," she'd said as they drove, spending much of the trip expounding on the history of the craft and on the amazing photos she'd seen online and in a book she'd found at the library.

Also as promised, no one had badgered her about a boyfriend or fiancé, and no one had tried to assign him that role. All in all, the day had been a great success.

Which was why he decided, in the loneliness of his bedroom, that he needed to stay away from Momi. She was too much—too beautiful, too kind, too smart, too compassionate, too . . . just about everything—for him to handle. He liked her more than any other woman he'd ever met, including his ex-wife, whom he'd thought himself in love with at the time of their marriage. When his marriage ended in dramatic fashion that Christmas Eve three years ago, he'd decided to stay away from future entanglements. Why endanger his heart again when he seemed so unable to detect a woman's true feelings? He could have a satisfactory life by doing what he enjoyed and keeping interactions with others to a minimum.

For three years his new philosophy had worked well. Now, he feared it was no longer enough. Was it already too late? Or could he preserve his new lifestyle and his carefree existence by keeping his distance from his upstairs neighbor?

Ruby lost no time in arranging to see Momi alone before she had to head back to Honolulu for Monday classes. She'd pulled her aside on Thanksgiving day, extracting a promise from Momi to meet for pizza on Friday afternoon. Momi knew she could take some personal time that afternoon. The library would not be busy; everyone would be shopping.

On Friday, Ruby barely gave Momi time to sit down before she was quizzing her about Rick.

"So, tell me all about him," she urged. "He's not nearly as old as you let on. I liked him."

Curious at this comment, Momi had to ask. "How old do you think he is?"

"Oh, I'd say early thirties. Why, what did you think?"

Momi shook her head. "I don't know. Maybe it's his attitude. At first I thought he was at least fifty, but I've been adjusting that downward as I've gotten to know him. Lately I've been thinking late thirties, forty maybe."

"That's not too old for a husband," Ruby said. Her

voice was definite. "He looked really nice too. You always call him a bum."

There was an accusation there, Momi thought. Ruby really *had* liked him.

"He cleaned up well. Really," she added as Ruby shot her another look. "It's the first time I've seen him clean-shaven. And wearing an Aloha shirt that wasn't completely faded out or stained or something."

"Have you met anyone else?"

"No," Momi admitted. "I meet people at work all the time, but it doesn't seem like any of those men could develop into a date or anything. Most of them have kids—that's why I meet them. So they're sure to have wives or significant others."

"They could be single dads," Ruby suggested. "But I still think there's a good chance Rick is the one Grandmother Helen picked out. What about dreams?"

"Jade told you about those?" Momi considered. She'd certainly had dreams, but so far she was getting nowhere on interpreting them. She'd even checked a book out of the library that purported to explain dreams and their meanings. "I have dreams, but they don't make any sense. There are no people in them—or anyway, no identifiable people. Just hazy forms that I can never really make out."

Ruby sighed. "That's too bad. It's been over a month since you got the quilt. Jade was engaged by then." But her enthusiasm quickly resurfaced. "What are the dreams about?"

Momi explained about the dinners she saw herself hostessing in her dreams. "So I thought that might mean I should learn to cook. You know Mom always said you have to be a good cook to get a husband."

"So, are you learning? That stuff you brought yesterday wasn't cooked, but it was absolutely amazing."

Momi grinned. "It's an ancient Thai craft, fruit and vegetable carving. I discovered it on the Internet. I spent hours doing the carving, but it's so much fun. It's crafts, but with food."

Momi talked about the fun she'd had making the edible flowers until their pizza arrived. Silence prevailed while the sisters tucked in.

But Ruby wasn't quiet for long. "So, are you taking cooking lessons?"

"Not real sign-up lessons," Momi said. "Rick is teaching me. He says you don't have to take classes, just be able to read and follow directions. So far I've made a roast chicken with mashed potatoes and green beans—we didn't do stuffing. And then I did a meat loaf. It was really good. Next time you're in town, I'll make it for you."

Ruby couldn't contain her mirth. She almost whooped with joy, then clapped a hand over her mouth. She looked around the room to be sure she hadn't disturbed everyone in the place.

"Oh, Momi, for sure he's the one. It's too romantic, his teaching you to cook."

But Momi shook her head. "We're just friends, Ruby,

really. Three weeks ago I never would have believed it possible. I was so mad about the plumbing, and I was convinced he was just a beach bum and probably not too smart." She took a bite and chewed thoughtfully. "But he's more complicated than I first thought. Still, I don't see it going beyond friendship. We're too different. He has no ambition at all, and I think that's important in a man. He's in his thirties and content to manage a small apartment complex and bum around the beach." She shook her head, still amazed that anyone could aspire to so little. "And he's kind of secretive about personal stuff, so there might be something bad there. He never talks about himself. I don't know where he's from or what he did before he became an apartment manager here in Kona. Nothing."

Ruby laughed. "Ah, a mysterious past. Face it, the curiosity is killing you."

Momi laughed too. Rick did arouse her curiosity. It was such a challenge trying to get information out of him, one she had yet to meet. Still . . .

"He's just a friend," she reiterated. "It's nice to have a friend in the building."

Rick tried to keep busy in the days after Thanksgiving. He needed activities to keep him caught up and away from his upstairs neighbor. He was getting too involved in her life, too interested in everything about her.

How had he gotten himself into this situation? Three years ago he'd embarked on a new life, a decision he had never once regretted. But a large part of that new life plan had included keeping his distance from women like Momi Kanahele. He wanted to take things less seriously, to have fun. To stay away from things that might start him back on that road to high blood pressure and ulcers that he had so easily abandoned. To protect his heart from the kind of hurt his ex had managed to cause.

He'd had girlfriends since his move. But he'd been very careful, choosing young women on vacation looking for a little fun, or older women who enjoyed the same things he did but were not looking for commitment.

But right from the first, he'd known Momi was different. Something about her had immediately set his radar on alert. Even though he did not meet her face-to-face for months, he'd been very aware of her and her movements. It was a crying shame that her plumbing had given out on Halloween. They might have gone on for years living as neighbors with a mere nodding acquaintance.

Rick heaved a sigh as a lovely tourist wearing a string bikini strolled by his beach chair. She threw him a look that could definitely lead somewhere. And he wasn't even tempted.

He pulled his hat brim down lower and stared at the paperback novel in his hands. It was the latest thriller that every other person on the beach seemed to be reading, yet he couldn't recall a single thing about either the plot or the characters.

He slammed the book shut, not even bothering to mark his place. He'd have to start over anyway.

With another massive sigh, he gathered up his things and headed back to the apartment. He'd try some fishing. Much more private. He'd take his iPod too. Listening to music might let him leave some of his more bothersome thoughts behind. He needed to relax. And a fish dinner would be a nice bonus.

Darn that Momi. She'd put a serious dent in his new lifestyle. It was hard to devote himself to a fun and carefree existence when all he could do was think of her.

Deciding not to see Momi and actually following through on that promise were two completely different things.

Suddenly Momi was everywhere.

When he left his apartment for the beach on Friday morning, there she was, in the hall above him, hanging a wreath on her door. He assumed she left for work at some point. But when he came in from his errands that evening, there she was again, wrapping garlands made of local greenery around the stair railings. As he frowned at her, she rushed up the stairs, returning quickly with another wreath.

"I made this for you," she told him. "I didn't think you'd bother yourself, and it's not very festive without decorations."

Rick frowned at her. "All this stuff you're draping around . . ." He gestured toward the stairwell. "It's a fire hazard. Those greens are going to turn brown pretty quickly, you know. Then all it will take is one careless toss of a cigarette butt."

Momi frowned back at him. But her frown was thoughtful, not angry.

"I hadn't thought of that." She sighed, as though already picturing the stairs without her garlands. Then her face brightened. "But lots of places use greens at this time of year, and they don't seem to worry about fire. After all, it's just a few weeks. I'll bring my spray bottle out every day and spritz them. That will help."

But Rick was shaking his head slowly from side to side.

"Most places use fake greenery," he said.

"Oh." For a moment she appeared daunted. But her eyes quickly brightened. "I don't see why that would make such a difference. That fake stuff has to be as much of a fire hazard as this." She waved toward her decorations, her face showing her pride in what she'd done.

It did look nice, Rick admitted—but only to himself.

"The fake stuff is treated for fire resistance."

"Oh. I didn't think of that," Momi said.

Once again, Rick watched as her eyes lost their sparkle.

"I guess I should have realized." She heaved a great sigh. "Okay. I'll take this all down as soon as it dries out. Maybe I'll be able to get some fake stuff to replace it, but I don't think it will be as nice. The fake stuff doesn't have the nice smell," she added, taking a deep breath.

Rick knew what she meant. The smell of pine took him right back to Christmases of his youth. Unfortunately, it also took him back three years ago to the worst night of his life. The one thing he didn't mind about Momi's garlands was the fact that they did not have a traditional pine scent. In Hawaii almost everything was evergreen, so there was no reason to use only pine and cedar for decorating. The locally grown Christmas trees were not Scotch pines or Douglas firs. They were usually some type of juniper, or Norfolk Island pines with their widely spaced branches.

The greenery Momi was so carefully draping over the stair railings seemed to be composed of just about everything that grew on the island. He imagined she must have picked bits and pieces from gardens all over town, then twisted or plaited it all together the way *wili* or *hili* style leis were made. There was some juniper but many other kinds of leaves, buds, seeds, and even a few flowers. More than he would ever be able to identify. And it smelled fresh and outdoorsy, blending nicely with the scent of the nearby ocean.

Rick looked at her solemnly. "Not everyone is a Christian, you know."

Momi appeared stricken. He could tell from her expression that it hadn't occurred to her that not everyone in the building might celebrate Christmas.

"Oh, I'm sorry. Did one of the other residents complain? I feel really bad. I thought everyone here *did* celebrate Christmas. I know that not everyone in the islands is a Christian, of course, but I just didn't think . . ."

She stopped and took a deep breath. "I guess I just didn't think. I'm so sorry. Please tell me who it is so that I can apologize personally. I didn't mean any harm. I just enjoy the holidays so much, especially decorating."

Rick knew he was stuck now, because no one *had* complained. And while there were a lot of islanders who practiced the Buddhist or Shinto religions, he didn't know if any of his tenants were members. He just liked to set her off; he liked the way her eyes sparkled when she got upset, and the way she stood up to him and for herself.

But if there had been a complaint about her decorations, she did have a right to learn who made it, because he knew she was sincere about apologizing for any discomfort she had created. It was the kind of thing Momi took seriously, and she wouldn't rest until she made sure things were all right.

He couldn't just ignore her request, not with her so apologetic and sorry. She looked sad enough to cry. Seeing her that way gave him an odd feeling in his chest, as though a hand had wrapped around his heart and squeezed. Suddenly he was sorry that he was playing around with her.

"It's not any of the tenants."

She stared at him for a moment in confusion—then her eyes cleared, and she began to apologize profusely.

"Oh, Rick, I'm so sorry. I didn't realize. It's the Irish name, of course."

It was his turn to stare at her in confusion. "What are you talking about?"

"You're Jewish, aren't you? I'm so sorry. . . ."

Rick was shaking his head.

"Okay, okay. I admit it." He raised his hands, palms out, as though warding her off. "No one complained. I just didn't want any Christmas decorations out here. I've told you before, I don't like the holidays, and I especially don't like Christmas."

Momi just looked at him, as if she couldn't comprehend someone who didn't celebrate with joy at holiday time.

"And I like to get you riled," he admitted, somewhat on the sheepish side now. He shrugged. "I like to see the way your eyes sparkle with anger, and the way your chest heaves with the breaths you take trying to control yourself." He raised his eyebrows up and down in a comic, leering pose.

Momi stared at him, startled. "You . . ."

She didn't know what to say. With one last look toward Rick, she turned and ran up the stairs.

Momi was terribly confused. She had had a wonderful time at Clarice's with Rick and her family. And she was sure he had too. The food had been wonderful, and her relatives had all treated him as one of them. She'd thought the day had firmed up their friendship. With her local friendships disrupted by her years away at school, she was happy to have a friend so close by. She'd come to enjoy her time with Rick and found herself relying on him when she needed help. It was hard to believe how bad he'd been at helping her at that first fateful meeting. In fact, the story of that disastrous encounter with the exploding faucets had become a funny story that she recounted to others.

However, there was still the troublesome matter of the chemistry between them. She tried hard to ignore it. Rick showed no signs of having the same problem. Except for the way his eyes sometimes sparkled when he looked at her, he didn't seem to be affected at all by her presence.

Now to learn that he enjoyed getting her riled . . . And that indication that he liked to do it because of her physical response. She crossed her arms over her chest in an instinctive reaction.

She just didn't know what to do about the irritating man. How could anyone hate Christmas and all the wonderful decorations that went with it?

The beginnings of a smile played over her lips as she thought of how she might be able to remedy such uncommon ideas. She did love a challenge.

For now, though, she retreated to her own apartment. She was making wreaths for everyone in the building, and she was only half-done. She didn't know all the tenants yet, but she thought it would be a nice way to meet them. And to decorate the complex too.

And, just in case Rick was correct about everyone's

not celebrating a Christian holiday, she made sure that hers were religion-neutral, containing nothing but local greenery and colorful ribbons.

Once again, *pahu* drums interrupted her dream. She was at the apartment complex this time. It was her apartment building, and yet it wasn't, in that strange way things change when they appear in dreams. She was decorating for Christmas, stringing garlands and lights and hanging wreaths. But as quickly as she put the things up, Rick came along and took them down. She worked faster, but so did he.

Then a tin of cookies appeared in her hand. From it she took gingerbread men threaded with string and hung them among the garlands and from trees in the apartment building's atrium. This new action seemed to calm the panicked rush. Rick took some cookies, but instead of hanging them, he ate them. Still, the atmosphere had changed. She was no longer having trouble breathing as she continued hanging her decorations. She felt good. She was happy that Rick liked her cookies. And the tin seemed bottomless.

And then the drums started, waking her up before she could see what would happen next. Except that they weren't drums at all. Someone was pounding on her door. Again.

She blinked at the clock, trying to see what time it was. Someone was banging on her door at seven in the morning. On her day off! It had to be Rick. Who else would be making such a racket so early in the morning? All the rest of her friends knew she liked to sleep in.

Realizing that he would not stop until she got up and opened the door, Momi pushed back the covers and got out of bed. This time she remembered to pull on a robe before heading for the door.

She flung it open without even bothering with the peephole. She'd know that knock anywhere.

"What is it this time?"

"My, my, aren't we grumpy in the morning? And here I am, playing Santa Claus."

Momi's eyes widened with surprise. Rick was holding a gorgeous specimen of a Christmas tree. It was a deep, healthy green, a smidgen taller than he was and beautifully shaped. It was a mainland tree, too, a fine-looking Douglas fir. Momi knew those could be quite pricey, as they were shipped in from the northwest. Where had he gotten it?

"You brought me a tree?" She blinked. "A *real* tree?"

The scent of pine washed over her, heightening her already high Christmas spirit. She took a deep breath, half closing her eyes in pleasure.

"It was a gift. And you know how I feel about Christmas trees."

Momi smiled. "Fire hazards."

"Yeah. So I thought maybe you'd like it. I didn't want to hurt their feelings by turning it down."

"Oh, no, you couldn't do that."

Momi's smile refused to go away. She was too happy for words. The tree was truly wonderful. She couldn't wait to start decorating it. And Rick was showing his soft side again. A real curmudgeon wouldn't worry about hurting someone else's feelings.

"They won't be coming to visit and see that you don't have a tree in your apartment?"

"Not a chance."

Momi moved back, allowing Rick and the tree access. She almost asked why someone close enough to give him such an excellent gift would not be invited into his place in the coming month. But knowing how closemouthed he could be about personal matters, she decided to let it go. For now.

"It's got a stand and everything," Rick said, carrying the tree inside. Its branches folded back as he came through the door, dropping some needles and exuding more of its delectable aroma.

"How about in front of the window here?"

"Perfect."

"Just go on in and change. I'll make sure it's straight, then leave you to it."

Still smiling, Momi retreated into her bedroom. Her eyes were immediately drawn to the red and white quilt; it had been pulled up over her as she slept. And she'd had that strange dream.

Was Grandmother Helen trying to tell her something? But what? If she was hoping to let her know that Rick was antagonistic toward holiday decorations, she already knew that. On the other hand, he was in her living room right now, setting up a lovely Christmas tree, one much nicer than any she could have afforded to buy herself. So his good deed this morning negated any message she could see in that part of the dream.

Straightening the bedclothes, Momi debated the meaning of the dream. Were people just better at interpreting dreams back in her ancestor's day? If only Grandmother Helen could speak to her directly. Her mother claimed that Helen had returned to her husband in a dream, telling him to give the quilt to their daughter when she finished school and was old enough to be married. Why couldn't she speak to *her* in such a clear-cut manner?

At least the second part of the dream seemed more clear cut. Perhaps cookies were the way to this man's heart. She'd seen cookies hanging on Christmas trees; she even liked the look of it. But she'd never made anything but chocolate chip cookies. It might be time to try something new.

With a shake of her head, Momi discarded her robe and pulled on her jeans and a red shirt. She smiled as she imagined Rick's reaction to the *Ho! Ho! Ho!* printed discreetly in white across the front.

Rick was still fussing with the tree when she came back out. He'd put on coffee, too, and the last of it was dripping into the pot. The mingling aromas of coffee brewing and Christmas pine was overwhelming. Momi breathed deep, happiness flooding through her.

"I think I've found the best side for you," Rick said, still critically examining the tree.

Momi's heart turned over. No matter how much he might try to irritate her about the holiday and her decorating, he really cared about the appearance of the tree. Warmth flowed through her as she realized that it had to be because he cared about her.

"You have to stay and help with the decorating," she said, pouring out two mugs of coffee.

But Rick was shaking his head before she even finished the sentence.

"Uh-uh. I don't do Christmas."

Momi rolled her eyes, handing him one of the mugs. She might as well offer a suitably juvenile reply to his stubborn stance.

"You claimed not to do Thanksgiving either, but you had a good time at Auntie Clarice's. I know you did. Everyone enjoyed your company too."

"I don't like holidays," he said.

"Yeah," she said. "I know."

She raised the mug to her lips but stopped short of sipping. Steam rose from the surface of the liquid, hitting her lip with a warning she decided to heed.

"I had a dream last night where I was decorating the building, and you were tearing things down as fast as I could put them up."

A smile softened his lips. "Dreaming again, huh?"

"I don't suppose you know anything about interpreting dreams?"

Rick looked at her hopeful face and hated to disappoint her. Still, he was fighting for his own well-being here. So he grinned.

"I can tell you what *that* dream means. It means I hate Christmas." He waggled his eyebrows, hoping to make her laugh.

But if Momi noticed, she chose to ignore it. Instead, she waved a hand over her cup, turning away from him to concentrate on the tree. It was a cute gesture, but he didn't think it would help cool her drink any. And it didn't look as if she was going to address his comment either.

"This is my first apartment, you know. I always had a roommate before. And of course, I always went home for Christmas."

"Of course," Rick muttered. Anyone who had spent every Thanksgiving of her life with her family would certainly have spent every Christmas with them too.

Once again, Momi chose to ignore his comment. She continued as though he had not spoken.

"I planned on a small tree."

Finally she turned toward him, taking a sample sip from her mug. It must have been the proper temperature, because she smiled and took another. Rick raised his cup. Just right.

"I won't have nearly enough ornaments for such a

large tree. So you'll have to help me." Momi smiled at him.

Rick melted at that smile. Happiness flowed from her—in her expression, in the leashed excitement of her movements.

He kept his voice as unemotional as possible. "I told you, I don't do Christmas."

Rick attempted to frown, but he wasn't sure the expression made it onto his face. The panic he felt at the sensations flooding him might have. Momi did give him a strange look. But her enthusiasm didn't flag for long.

"Okay," she said, the happy smile back in place. "I'll put all the things on the tree myself. But you can help get things ready. Stringing popcorn, for instance."

Suddenly she twirled, hurried into the kitchen, and pulled open a cupboard. Then another. "Darn. No popcorn."

She turned a bright smile toward him. "Why don't you run to the store for me while I get out my decorations? Get me some popcorn and cranberries."

As she gave Rick her shopping list, he noticed a strange expression that was quickly replaced with something akin to cunning. What was going through that cute little head now? Her next words brought him no closer to solving the problem.

"I know. Let's see what we need to make gingerbread cookies," she said. "They would make nice decorations, don't you think?"

Rick hated to admit it, but her enthusiasm was

beginning to get to him. The thought of spending the afternoon with her, warm and cozy, stringing popcorn, with gingerbread in the oven . . . It was very appealing. It even made him think of childhood Christmases—long before the bad stuff moved in and messed with his head.

"Okay."

His simple agreement brought out a smile so full of happiness and light, he wanted to go over to her, wrap her in his arms, and kiss her until he forgot all about his ex and his dysfunctional family.

Instead, he nodded briefly and turned toward the door.

"I'll check online for a recipe. How much popcorn do you want?"

By lunchtime, Momi had strung lights on the tree, using every string of colored lights she owned, including several she'd meant to use in her windows. Rick had been to the store and back, popping several bowls worth of corn. They sat together on the floor, pushing kernels onto needles to create the long strings needed for the tree. Every few inches, they added a cranberry to the mix, giving the popcorn strings a cheerful touch of color.

"It's a shame I don't have more lights," Momi said, popping a kernel into her mouth and frowning at the tree.

"Looks fine to me," Rick said. He pulled his needle off, the long thread in his hands now completely filled. He'd never seen a tree decorated with real popcorn.

"Let's see how this looks," he said, approaching the tree with the string of popped corn in his hands. He draped it over several of the branches and stepped back to assess his handiwork. "Not bad."

Momi almost held her breath. Despite his adamant insistence about not celebrating Christmas, and definitely not decorating, he'd just added a string of popcorn and cranberries to her tree.

"It looks terrific," she said. She didn't want to scare him off by saying too much about his participation. "Let's have some lunch, and then we can make the gingerbread men. We can continue to string popcorn while we wait for the cookies to bake."

Rick was agreeable. "Sewing popcorn is easier than it sounds," he said. "It's sure easier than sewing on a button."

"You can sew on buttons?" Momi's voice echoed her surprise.

But it didn't faze Rick. His voice as he replied was matter-of-fact. "Sure. I'm a man living alone. I can cook and do laundry and vacuum. And I can sew on a button."

"Good for you. Lots of guys just talk a girlfriend into doing that kind of thing."

Rick shrugged. He went to a cupboard and pulled out some chips to go with the turkey sandwiches she was putting together. Then he took two cans of passion-orange-guava from the refrigerator.

"You're a good man to have around," Momi told him as she brought the sandwiches to the table. Rick already had everything else in place.

He just grinned at her—that heart-stopping grin that brought out his dimple and made her knees weak.

Momi took a deep breath before biting into her sandwich. "The tree smells so good," she said.

"We always had Douglas firs when I was a kid."

Momi tried to hide her surprise at this shared bit of childhood trivia, concentrating on holding her look of mild interest. Rick *never* talked about himself or his family. So she remained silent, hoping he would go on.

"Funny, how scents can take you back." Rick turned his eyes toward the tree. "I never saw the tree being decorated. My mother always did it while I was at school. She probably thought I'd get in her way."

Momi's heart ached for a little boy who had never been allowed to help decorate the family Christmas tree. Tree decorating with her family was one of her most cherished holiday memories.

"That's a shame," she finally said, hoping her voice was nonjudgmental. "My family always did it together. It was a lot of fun."

"My mother's way was okay," Rick said. "Walking in from school and seeing that tree all decorated was really something. I'd know it would be there as soon as I walked in and smelled the fresh pine. It was pretty special, leaving the house in the morning when it looked just as usual, then coming in to the lights and glitter and a fabulous tree."

Rick looked at the cardboard carton Momi had brought out, the one filled with her Christmas ornaments.

There were paper trees and macaroni wreaths she'd made in grade school there, and felt animals and painted wooden ornaments she'd done as a teenager and adult.

"We didn't have ornaments with such personal associations. My mother liked everything just so, and themed trees. She used glass balls and strings of tinsel and beads. Some years everything was white, some years mixed colors. One year she did an all pink tree, and I hated it on sight."

Momi grinned. He must have been young, and all boy, to hate a pink tree so heartily.

"Anyway, I never knew what to expect, so it was always a surprise."

Momi thought she might have shown some of her dismay when he blinked and looked away.

"I'm sure these ornaments are nicer," he said. "They must be full of memories."

"They are. But your mother's trees sound beautiful. She must have had a lot of ornaments to be able to specialize that way."

Rick shrugged.

They were both surprised by an insistent knock on her door.

Momi went over, checked the peephole, and opened the door. She recognized Naomi, another woman who lived in the apartment building.

"Rick," the new arrival said right away. "I'm so glad I found you. My toilet is stopped up, and the plunger didn't work. Could you come over?"

So off he went, responsibilities regarding the apartments having to come before recreational time with another tenant.

Darn, Momi thought. And just as he was opening up about himself, too. How much more might she have learned if not for the old plumbing in the building?

Chapter Nine

Rick awoke from a sound sleep. Reluctantly. He'd been at the beach with Momi, lying side by side on matching towels. She was a delicious sight in her deep blue bikini. If he'd only stayed asleep another five minutes, he might have been smoothing sunblock onto the satiny skin of her back.

What had awakened him, anyway? It was still dark.

He rolled over, squinting at the clock. Before the time even registered, he heard a muffled pounding on his door. That was what woke him. He recognized that sound too. It was a small female fist trying hard to make a lot of noise. In other words, it was Momi herself, trying to rouse him but not the rest of the building. Considerate of her. But he was sure she would *not* be wearing a bikini, blue or any other color.

With a sigh, he pushed himself out of bed, combed his fingers through his hair, and pulled on the surfer shorts lying on the floor. He arrived at the door just as another series of thumps rumbled through the apartment.

Rick pulled the door wide, putting his arms out as Momi almost fell through the opening. "What?"

His voice was harsh, raspy from allergies first thing in the morning. He knew most people thought it was because he drank. Just because he was a bachelor and didn't have a traditional job. He frowned at Momi, wondering what *she* thought.

She stepped back and away from him, straightening her shoulders as though gathering her strength. And being particularly careful not to look at his bare chest.

"Don't tell me you've got another problem." His glance took her in from head to toes. "You're not wet at least." He gave her his classic eyebrow waggle.

Momi glared at him, pushing her hair away from her face even though it was already caught back in a clip.

"This is serious, Rick. It's not an accident—I mean, not like you think. This is a different kind of emergency."

He remained standing in the doorway, awaiting an explanation. Nothing was forthcoming. She just shifted from foot to foot and bit at her lower lip.

After the dream he'd been having, seeing the white edge of her teeth press on her full bottom lip was enough to be disconcerting. So he made an effort to concentrate on her eyes.

She looked worried.

"What happened?" he asked. That anxious expression always got him right in the solar plexus, making him want to protect her, to help make things better.

"It's my other chaperone. I'm taking a group of the library kids to the mountain, to see the snow. Remember, I told you we were going the Friday after Thanksgiving? But there wasn't any snow then, so the trip was postponed. My associate was supposed to go with me to chaperone, only Charlie called a few minutes ago. He's got the flu. Was up all night, uh, you know."

Rick wondered what she would say if he claimed not to know. The thought brought a smile to his lips—just enough to quirk them to one side.

Momi found herself staring at his lips. He was smiling—one of those crooked smiles that Elvis Presley was so famous for. Not that she'd ever found anything special about the so-called king. And though she was born after his death, she'd seen plenty of film footage of Elvis, her grandmother's all-time favorite. But on Rick . . . wow!

The half smile, sending just the right side of Rick's lips upward, did something unsettling to Momi's breathing pattern. If that's what the Elvis smile had done for his fans, she could finally understand their eternal devotion.

"So . . ." she heard Rick say.

"Hmm?"

She pulled her gaze away from his mouth and managed to remember why she was standing in his doorway at five-fifty in the morning.

"Ah, well." Still hesitant to broach the subject that had her standing at his door at such an early hour, she flew on with the explanation. "He wanted to come anyway, so I wouldn't have to cancel the trip, but I told him he can't expose all the kids to the flu. And the bus I rented doesn't have a bathroom."

Rick nodded solemnly. "An important consideration."

Once again Momi noticed the twitch at the corner of his mouth. She had the impression that he wanted to laugh at her but was controlling the impulse.

"I, uh, tried calling a couple of other people," she continued, "and I may have lost at least one friend from the way he was yelling at me for calling so early." She sighed. "But no one else can go today. So I'm desperate."

Rick continued to stare at her, a small, upward, slanting quirk to his lips giving the impression that he was amused by the whole thing. She would just have to come out and ask.

"I wondered if you could possibly go with me."

She rushed on, hoping to delay his refusal long enough for him to reconsider. "We have to have at least two adults, you see, because of insurance, and I can't find anyone else who can make it today. You're my last chance to salvage the trip. The kids were really looking forward to it too."

She put on her most pitiful look, hoping for a puppy-dog expression that would convince him to go.

Rick shook his head. "Go ahead, put a guy on the spot, why don't you?"

He looked into her eyes, and she blinked rapidly a few times, as though trying to stop tears.

He sighed. "Sure, I can go."

Before she could launch herself at him for a joyful hug, he frowned mightily. "But only because you're in such a tight spot. You got it?"

"Of course."

She held herself back, bouncing in place as she worked hard not to leap into the air. "Thank you, thank you. We have to leave in half an hour. I'll meet you right here in twenty minutes."

She turned and raced up the stairs.

Once inside her apartment, she closed the door and leaned against it, taking several deep breaths.

Good grief, if she hadn't gotten out of there *right that minute,* she probably would have kissed him. Just thrown her arms around him, bare chest and all, and planted a kiss right on his appealing lips.

But the worst part was that it had less to do with gratitude for his last-minute help than with the way he looked. His eyes had that hooded look of someone just awakened from beautiful dreams, and his mouth was crooked at just the proper angle. Her insides felt all scrambled, and her heart pounded.

She supposed some of that could be blamed on the way she'd run up the stairs. Except it was already beating double-time even before she'd touched her foot to the first step.

Momi took another deep breath and pushed away from the door. She was in deep trouble.

Rick couldn't believe he was chaperoning a group of schoolchildren up the mountain. When he left mainland life behind, he'd decided he didn't care if he never spent another day in cold, dreary, winter weather. He'd dumped all his winter gear, along with his business suits and his type-A lifestyle.

So what the heck was he doing driving up the mountain toward that white stuff that fell way too low on the summit? Getting ready to freeze his—he glanced around at the kids and stopped himself from even thinking the word. He sighed.

Luckily, Momi had an odd assortment of winter clothing, including a coat big enough for his large frame. She said they were donations from friends and relatives who went to college in areas where there was snow, then returned to Hawaii. Rick was grateful, as he had no desire to get frostbite because he was too smitten with his enthusiastic neighbor to just say no.

Rick had had to smile when he saw their transportation. "No bathroom on the bus" indeed. Their transport was no tour bus, but an old school bus, its yellow paint faded from years in the tropical sun.

Still, the ride might have been fun if he'd been able to sit beside Momi on the narrow seat. With the road conditions, there would have been more than enough bouncing to push them together again and again. But she'd assigned him a place across from the driver, next to the door, then proceeded to the back, where she'd had the children put the bags of winter clothes.

After ten minutes on board, Rick began to wish for some aspirin. After twenty minutes, he wondered what might be more powerful than aspirin—and wished he had some of that.

The children chattered noisily—loudly—the entire way. Most of them had never seen snow up close and personal, so the air was thick with excitement. He wanted to tell them that it wasn't worth all this exuberance, but then his memories kicked in. Childhood memories of sledding down the hill in the park. Skating on the frozen pond. Building snowmen and snow forts. Snowball fights.

Yeah, snow might be a bane to adults, but it was pure joy to children.

He turned in his seat, looking into the eager faces behind him. Time to take his chaperoning responsibilities seriously.

"We're almost there. You kids have enough clothes on for the cold?"

Momi had been walking up and down the aisle for the past twenty minutes, passing out coats, hats, and mittens.

A chorus of yells and cheers was the response. They might not have any sleds or saucers, but they were eager to have fun and share a new experience.

And suddenly, Rick understood Momi's appeal. It was the childlike joy she found in everyday things. *That* was the quality in her that made Rick want to wrap her in his arms and protect her. She could find such happiness in decorating a stairwell, in baking cookies. This morning was the first time he'd seen her with children, but it was instantly apparent how popular she was among this crowd. She reacted to things on their level, yet she never lapsed into childish behavior. She was always the responsible adult with them, but he could see that they were able to relate in a special way.

In fact, everyone finally quieted down when the bus stopped and Momi moved to the front to announce the plans for the day. They would spend two hours, she told them, unless the majority wanted to leave sooner.

"Not everyone likes the cold, remember," she said. "That's why so many people move here to Hawaii."

After playing in the snow, they would stop at a park for sandwiches and cookies. This was greeted with a loud cheer, which increased in volume when Rick got the signal to open the door, and everyone piled out.

It didn't take long for a snowball fight to break out. What kid, even in Hawaii, hadn't seen movies of people flinging snowballs at one another? Rick held back, still hoping to keep an emotional distance from Momi's project. Until she threw a handful of snow that hit him right in the face.

All the kids laughed uproariously. Rick wanted to return the favor, but he hesitated. Momi had told him that most of the kids came from broken homes, and he didn't want to do anything that might smack of bullying behavior. Who knew how many might have experienced that kind of thing in their home life?

But when Rick's eyes met Momi's, the laughter quickly drained from hers. Her cheeks were pink with the cold and her excitement, her lips a deep plum. Her eyes twinkled with merriment—until they met Rick's and deepened with pure emotion. And Rick no longer wanted to bean her with a snowball. He wanted to wrap his arms around her and kiss her until neither of them had breath left in their bodies. He knew she was feeling the same connection between them, and it was so hot, he was surprised the snow around them didn't melt to slush.

They might have been standing there still, their eyes locked in passionate but silent communication, if a low-flying plane hadn't intruded on the moment. Rick knew he hadn't been aware of anything or anyone else in those few seconds that seemed to last for minutes. All the children could have disappeared, and he wouldn't have had a clue where they'd gotten to. Luckily, they were all still there, in the snow around them, when he finally looked around as the plane continued its flight toward Hilo.

Most of the children had progressed from snowballs to building snowmen. Momi and Rick got involved too, and soon everyone was working together to create a monster of a snow creature.

The two hours passed quickly, with no one complaining of the cold. No one complained when it was time to leave, either, which Rick thought spoke for itself.

As Rick settled into his seat on the bus, which he thought was almost as bad as an airline seat, comfort-wise, he couldn't help thinking back to that special moment during the snowball fight. That extraordinary instant when their eyes met across the heads of several little bodies. He'd noticed before that the sizzle between him and Momi was growing and seemed to be getting hotter. What he'd seen today was that immediately after that emotionally charged look, Momi acted shyer, more reserved. He knew that if the children had not been all around them, he would have kissed her then. And it would not have been a peck on the cheek. With the way she'd been acting, Rick thought she knew it too.

Was he ready for the responsibility of a relationship with a woman like Momi? A woman who had *wife and mother* practically stamped on her forehead?

Rick hunkered down in his seat, frowning, for the entire trip back to Kona.

Momi was back to her normal self when they returned to the apartment house later that afternoon.

"Thank you so much, Rick," Momi said, stopping with him outside the door to his place. "I really owe you. Why don't you come over for dinner? I've been practicing my cooking. I got some recipes from my Grandma Lucas, and I made a pot of Portuguese red bean soup the other day. It turned out really well, and it's the kind of soup that tastes even better warmed up. And I have a loaf of bread my mom gave me—made fresh yesterday morning."

"Homemade soup and fresh bread, huh?" He grinned, and his dimple winked at her. "You twisted my arm. I've never tried baking bread, but there's nothing like home-made."

Momi grinned back. That dimple of his just made her melt. Especially after the day they'd had. He'd been so good with the kids. He was fun, but he also knew how to set limits and explain them in a way that children could understand. She didn't approve of controlling kids through fear of punishment.

"Maybe we could try it together one of these days," she said.

Rick raised his eyebrows, his lips parted in a wide grin, his dimple flashing at her.

She could feel the heat in her cheeks. What had she said?

"Making bread."

She imagined that bright patches of red stained her cheeks and thought that she didn't have to worry about his leering at her now.

"It might be fun to make bread," she continued, realizing she was babbling but afraid to stop in case she made an even bigger fool of herself. "I got Grandma Lucas' recipe for Portuguese sweet bread too. There's nothing like a loaf fresh from the oven."

Rick continued to grin. "Sounds like a plan," he said.

He reached into his pants pocket, removing the ring of keys that included his apartment door key. "You might catch a husband yet," he told her. "Your cooking is shaping up."

Momi's eyebrows flew upward at least an inch. "'Catch a husband'? What kind of comment is that?"

Uh-oh. Rick knew at once that he'd hit a nerve. There went his dreams of a cozy evening with her after their soup dinner. "Sorry, I didn't mean to offend you."

He tried to keep his voice casual, but that seemed to inflame her even more. "Isn't that what most women want? To get married and have a family?"

He stopped her sputtering before she managed to form any coherent words. "Hey, I'm just telling it like it is. You admitted you wanted me to go to your family Thanksgiving dinner so that the others wouldn't keep after you about getting married."

Momi frowned. She did want a husband and a family. And her relatives *would* have gotten after her about her lack of a boyfriend if not for Rick's presence. But it sounded so callous the way he said it. So calculating.

"I'm sure whether or not I can cook will not make any difference when I find my true love," she said. Her voice seemed incredibly haughty, but she barely cared. She was starting to regret asking him to eat with her.

"Don't kid yourself," he said. "It's going to make a big difference." He grinned at her. "Your 'true love,' huh? Man, I think you may be reading too many of those romance novels."

"I read very widely," she informed him, her voice still more haughty than not. But she wouldn't stand for his disparaging her reading material. "I do read romance novels, but I also read mysteries and biographies and history. . . ."

"Don't forget cookbooks," he added, his dimple once again slitting his cheek.

Momi thought he was trying to embarrass her again and even wondered briefly if he was trying to flirt with her. But she refused to let him get to her.

"Yes, thank you, cookbooks. Some of those have very informative material in them, about the origins of various foods and food's significance in particular ethnic cultures."

Her answer didn't elicit any response from Rick. He merely stood with the keys in his hand, grinning maddeningly at her.

Realizing that she was tired of this discussion, she moved toward the stairs. "If you still want to join me for soup, I'll see you at six," she said. "Otherwise, have a nice evening."

Then she turned and flounced up the stairs.

Momi took a long, hot shower. In the mountain cold, her inadequately shod feet in the snow, she'd longed for the steamy water and the warmth it would bring. Now, however, thoughts of Rick alone were almost enough to warm her.

As she stepped out of the bathroom, her warmest

robe wrapped around her, she looked at *Ka Makani Ka`ili Aloha*. Several generations of women in her family believed that it literally "wafts love from one to another." She believed in it too—she really did.

However, she had also believed in the swiftness of Grandmother Helen's work. But she'd had the quilt for over a month and still had not met her man. And though she'd had the dreams Jade told her to expect, they didn't explain anything.

As she pulled on her clothes, her mind kept turning over the dreams. Cooking, decorating . . . they had nothing to do with meeting her true love or with what would happen in her future life. The dreams were more confusing than anything.

She'd tried looking at a book on dream interpretation that she found at the library. But it was no help at all. She'd found that killing a turkey meant good luck was coming to you. But she hadn't *killed* the turkey in her dream; she'd just cooked it. That meant prosperity. At least it was somewhat the same thing. Other parts of the dream were contradictory. Dreaming of food was a good sign, she read; so was roasted food. But having a feast meant difficulties were on the horizon.

So she still didn't know what it was all supposed to mean.

She was learning to cook, if that's what Grandmother Helen had in mind. She wasn't cooking just for herself; that still wasn't very interesting. But she found that she loved to cook with Rick. Maybe she just needed the presence of other people to make it fun. Or she had to turn it into a creative, craftlike endeavor, like the sculpted fruit and vegetables that had been her contribution to the family Thanksgiving dinner.

As she combed out her hair, she couldn't help going back to that special moment in the snow, when she and Rick had looked into each other's eyes. What a great feeling that had been. She'd read about electricity connecting two people, but this was the first time she'd experienced it. The cold air had almost sparked with the heat of that look, and her insides had turned warm and sizzled. What might have happened if they hadn't been surrounded by a dozen children?

When she found herself staring into the mirror and not seeing a thing, she put down the brush and scolded herself for a silly fool. What was she doing? She didn't want to settle down with Rick. Why, they would spend half their time fighting with each other!

Realizing that she had donned her brand-new sweater, the rosy pink one that looked so good with her dark hair, she pulled it off. Her freshly combed hair was a complete mess again, but she'd find something else to wear.

Flipping through the sweaters in her drawer, she finally settled on an old blue one. It had been her favorite for a long time but was now pilled and therefore too grungy to wear to work. But it would do for dinner with Rick. She wouldn't want him to think she was dressing up, or—heaven forbid—trying to "catch a husband."

No, she definitely did not want Rick for a husband, no matter how great the chemistry was between them. She needed a husband she could look up to, someone who aspired to more than managing an apartment complex and lounging on the beach. She might be a fool for being such an intellectual snob, but she just could not reconcile herself to having a husband with no ambition at all.

She stopped with her hairbrush halfway through her curls as she reconsidered. Rick spoke too well to be uneducated. So she couldn't understand why he seemed content to be nothing more than a beach bum and general repairman at the apartment.

She remembered Ruby's suggestion that he might be on disability. But what would create enough of a problem to keep him from real work and yet leave no outward signs? Because he sure came across as a normal, healthy male.

Knowing she would never be able to solve the conundrum of Rick Mahoney before six o'clock, she decided to lie down for a few minutes. Folding back the quilt, Momi propped up her pillows and half sat, half reclined on the bed. Playing in the snow had proved tiring.

Momi started awake at six o'clock when there was a knock on her door. Surprised that she had actually fallen asleep, she was even more amazed to realize she'd been deep in a dream, the antique quilt pulled up to her chin. How had she done that, anyway, she wondered, as she glanced in the mirror, fluffing up her crushed hair. She was fully clothed in jeans and a sweater; she didn't feel at all cold, not now or before she'd fallen asleep.

She stood there for a moment, staring at the rumpled bed. The quilt's *mana* might be even more powerful than the family believed.

She called out to Rick that she was coming, so that she could take her time. She wanted to think about the new dream right now, while it was still clear in her mind.

This one had been a good dream—not upsetting or frustrating. She'd been in the kitchen again. Really, for a woman who previously didn't cook, all she did lately was dream of meals and cooking. Did her ancestor really think she had to learn how to cook, or was it a generational thing? In Helen Lovell's day, women had done all the cooking and housework, while men worked to support the family. But things had changed since then.

Unlike the other dreams, however, this one took place in a bright, cozy kitchen. She'd felt the peace and the love present in the room as she and a man made Christmas cookies. Unfortunately, she was never able to see the man's face. She just knew he was there, helping. Loving her. She thought there might have been children there, too, but she wasn't as sure about that.

But she did know that she and the man with her were deeply in love. If only she could have seen who it was! What good was it, having an ancestor who visited your dreams, if said ancestor couldn't "speak" to her in plainer terms?

Shaking her head, Momi walked toward the door.

"I'm coming!" she called again, so that Rick would know she was almost there. She wouldn't put it past him to open the door with his passkey if she was too slow about answering it.

Her mind was still busy digesting this most recent dream when she pulled open the door. And all thoughts of dreams fled. She was back in the present. A very nice present.

Rick stood there, wearing one of his nicer shirts, a bouquet of pink stargazer lilies in his hands.

"For you," he said, offering her the flowers with a small bow.

"For me?"

Momi's eyes rounded with surprise, then quickly sparkled with happiness. Rick's chest filled with a warm pleasure, glad of his ability to bring her joy.

"I love them!"

Momi stepped up to Rick, moving onto tiptoe to place an impetuous kiss on his cheek.

Rick's heart raced, and he had to take a deep breath to resist wrapping his arms around her and showing her what a *real* kiss could be.

"Mahalo," she said, stepping back and gesturing him inside. "Thank you," she repeated, looking up at him through her lashes in a shy yet seductive manner.

Rick took another steadying breath, watching her flit about the room.

"I have to put these in water," she said, glancing down at the flowers. "They're beautiful."

Rick watched her enthusiasm, thinking that her joy in his little surprise was more than worth the cost of the flowers. Her ability to pull so much happiness out of a small gesture was one of the main reasons he found her so appealing. And also the reason he felt she needed his protection. Surely she couldn't be as naive as she sometimes appeared.

"Did I wake you?" Rick asked. She'd seemed abstracted when she opened the door, as though just coming out of a trance.

Momi looked embarrassed.

"I thought I'd lie down for a minute, and I ended up napping. The trip was tiring—more so than I expected."

As she spoke, she took a vase from a cupboard and filled it with water, then added the flowers. She spent a few minutes longer clipping the stems and getting them just so. Then she walked around the counter to place them in the center of her dining table.

"They're beautiful. Thank you so much."

She stood beside the table, staring at them for a while before looking back at Rick. "They remind me of Halloween night."

If she'd said it with a laugh, Rick might have succumbed to desire and given her a quick kiss. But her eyes met his with a seriousness that made him want to take her into his arms and never let her go. More than ever, in fact, he wanted to kiss her. He wanted it so much, he knew he'd better not. Perhaps if they sat together, watching television after eating, as they had done once before. That might be the proper time to steal a kiss.

Rick broke eye contact, then decharged the atmosphere in the room with a bit of polite small talk.

"Something smells good." He looked toward the stove. "When you said you'd fallen asleep, I thought dinner would be late."

"Just like a man," Momi said. "Thinking of his stomach."

She headed back to the kitchen, opening the cupboard to get out the bowls.

"I put the pot on to warm before I went in to shower. It'll be ready anytime."

Chapter Ten

Rick liked Momi's soup well enough to have seconds. He had thirds of the bread, which she'd warmed to just-out-of-the-oven freshness in the microwave. He declared both recipes good additions to her new folder.

"Would you like to try Mom's bread recipe sometime?" Momi watched as Rick helped himself to the last piece. "It takes time to make, though, because you have to let it rise, then knead, and let it rise. . . . It takes all day."

"It might be a good activity for a rainy day."

Momi liked that idea. "Okay. The next rainy day that I have off, it's a date."

Once the food was gone, the leftovers stored away, and the dishes cleared, Momi led him into the adjoining room.

"It's been such a great winter day, let's watch *White Christmas*." She pulled a DVD from the shelf. "It's my favorite Christmas movie."

"You're kidding, right? I recall that as a really schmaltzy movie." He stepped forward to view the row of DVD boxes. When he finally turned back to her, he held another box in his hand.

"You really do go for the schmaltzy stuff, don't you? But you do have one thing worth watching." He held up the DVD box. "How about this?"

Momi looked at what he'd chosen. *The Lord of the Rings*.

"Oh, come on, Rick, be a big boy. I love Tolkien, and I love those movies, but not tonight. I want a Christmas movie."

Hearing the pleading behind her light tone, he acquiesced. Man, he was getting soft.

"Thanks," she said, granting him a happy smile that made it all worthwhile. "This will be as much fun as watching the game that time, remember?"

He remembered, all right. He'd suffered all night, sitting beside her, taking in that sweet floral scent that he had yet to identify. It was driving him mad. It wasn't gardenias, or *pikake*. He'd debated plumeria for some time, but now that he was beside her again, he didn't think that was it either. There were lots of different gingers in the islands—maybe one of those was what she used. He tried to recall if there had been any scent bottles in the bathroom that memorable Halloween night, but he drew a blank.

After a half hour of agony trying to keep his hands to himself, Rick gave up. He threw his arms across the back of the sofa, feeling like a kid trying to sneak a hug from his girl.

Minutes later, feeling all of sixteen, he lowered his arm from the back of the couch to Momi's shoulders. She was really into the movie, watching the singing and dancing with enjoyment. So much so, in fact, that she didn't seem to notice his arm around her at all. Within a minute, she'd leaned toward him, and in two minutes, she was snuggling her head against his shoulder.

With a smile of pleasure, Rick relaxed into the cushions. He could get used to this, he thought, running his palm along her arm. Her sweater was soft and worn, and the warmth of her body heated his hand, working its way into the rest of his system.

Yes, this was definitely nice. It would be even better, he thought, if they'd been watching his movie choice.

But even though he didn't enjoy *White Christmas* personally, the ending proved worthwhile. Momi sobbed through the sappy finish, when Bing Crosby and Danny Kaye held the surprise party for their retired general. Which gave him a chance to comfort her. And what better way to comfort a lovely woman than with a gentle kiss?

As the movie ended and the screen reverted to the menu, he slipped his arms around her, pulled her close, and dropped his head down to hers. His lips pressed lightly against hers. He almost expected an eruption of anger on her part, but she remained soft and pliant in his embrace. So he deepened the kiss.

And escaped into another world. The woman in his arms was wonderful—warm, sweet, and delightful in her inexperienced response. Holding her this way, savoring her unique taste, Rick could forget all the awful things he'd been through in the past. He felt that he could happily spend the entire night kissing her, and that the world around them would be a peaceful, beautiful place the whole while.

When he finally raised his head, Rick could barely focus on Momi's eyes. Her scent was all around him, the pleasant smells of pine tree and popcorn subsumed by that still-unidentified floral perfume. And he was so consumed with the feel and taste of her that his vision was temporarily blurred.

Momi, too, seemed to be having a problem. Her eyes looked so distracted and dreamy, he suspected she could not see at all.

Rick knew the exact moment when she came back to reality. She blinked, looked into his eyes, licked her lips, then pushed him away.

"What are you *doing?*" she said.

Rick laughed. He thought it probably too bad of him, but he couldn't help it. As some people had a piece of music that was "their" song, those words had to be "their" phrase; she must have used those particular words with him more than any others in the time they had known each other.

"I'm kissing you," he said with a final chuckle. "Isn't it obvious?"

Momi folded her arms over her chest. "Why?"

Rick raised his eyebrows. "Why? Because I'm a man. Because you're a woman."

He raised and lowered his eyebrows in his imitation of Groucho Marx's famous leer. That usually brought a smile, but Momi was never predictable. She frowned.

"And you're such an attractive woman," he added.

Momi looked at him for a long time without comment. He remained where he was, sitting on the sofa still but no longer close enough to touch her.

"And I like you."

He could usually read her expressions pretty well through her expressive eyes. Emotions flowed through them as freely as tears. But this evening, after he'd come the closest to commitment in years, that ability failed him. All he could see was stunned awe—and that made no sense at all. It couldn't be due to his kiss; he wasn't so egocentric as to think that he could overwhelm her with one kiss, even one as special as what they had just shared.

Finally she spoke. "I think you should leave now."

"Momi . . ." he began. And realized he had nothing he could really say to her. Wisecracks wouldn't work and at this point might even harm their relationship.

"Okay. Thank you for dinner. It was delicious. I'll see you tomorrow, okay?"

He noticed that she didn't acknowledge his parting comment. And he wasn't going to push. So he gathered up his self-respect, pulled it around him, and walked out, shutting the door quietly behind him.

Momi remained seated on the sofa, watching his back as he left. She noticed that, for once, he was standing tall. He looked very dignified.

As the door clicked softly shut, she dropped her head into her hands and took a deep breath. Somehow, she'd fallen for Rick. She didn't know how it could have happened. She'd decided some time ago that she liked him. As a friend. *Only* as a friend.

But that kiss had changed everything. The feelings that flowed through her when he held her in his arms . . . the powerful emotion that he drew from deep inside her . . .

Yes, no doubt about it, that kiss was the clincher.

Fumbling for the phone, Momi hit the speed dial.

"Ruby, I think you may be right."

Her sister never missed a beat, even though there wasn't a chance she knew what Momi was talking about.

"Great. I love being right."

Momi groaned.

"That bad, huh?" Ruby asked.

"You must be right about Rick. And the quilt."

Ruby waited for Momi to say more, but the pause lengthened.

"So," she finally said, "what happened?"

"Today was the snow trip for the library kids. Remember, I told you about it at Thanksgiving?"

Ruby murmured something Momi may or may not have heard.

"The other chaperone got sick—the flu—and I couldn't find anyone else to fill in. And I had to have two adults or cancel because of the library rules and insurance. So I asked Rick, and he went with me."

"Great," Ruby inserted.

"So afterward, I invited him up for dinner—to thank him, you know."

"Sounds fine so far," Ruby said. "It was really nice of him to go. Responsible, even."

"Yeah, but now I'm going crazy wondering what's happening between us. There was this moment on top of the mountain."

She was silent for a moment, remembering. The way their eyes met, the understanding that sizzled between them. She just knew that if all those kids hadn't been there, she would have been wrapped in his arms, returning his kisses. It was so desirable, it was downright scary.

"I'm telling you, Ruby, it was just like a movie. The kids were going wild all around us, throwing snowballs. And I threw a sorry excuse for a snowball that gave him a faceful of snow. But then our eyes met—that was the part like a movie. You know, when the background fades out and you just see the two people standing there staring into each other's eyes."

"Wow." Ruby breathed the word into the phone. "That is so beautiful."

"*Now* it is," Momi admitted. "At the time it scared me to death.

"And then he had dinner with you? What did you make?"

"He did come. I wasn't sure he would, because we'd had a disagreement after we got back. And he brought me flowers—because of that, I guess. But they were beautiful—stargazer lilies. Like the ones he got for my hair on Halloween."

"Wow," Ruby said once again. "I thought he was pretty nice when I met him, but now I know for sure this is a great guy. You'd be crazy to let him go, Momi."

"We had a good time this evening. I heated up the soup I made the other day—Portuguese red bean soup from Grandma Lucas' recipe."

Ruby made an appreciative noise. All the Kanahele girls loved Grandma Lucas' red bean soup.

"After dinner, we watched a movie. And he kissed me."

"Great."

"I don't know."

"How can you not know?" Ruby asked. Her voice clearly sent her impatience across to her sister.

"I already told you, it's making me crazy. He's all wrong for me. This might be the first time the quilt made a mistake."

"You have to give it a chance. I like Rick. He's a nice guy with a capital *N*. He went to Auntie Clarice's for

Thanksgiving, after all. He filled in for you today. Not too many beach bums would give up a day at the beach to chaperone a snow trip with a bunch of kids. I still don't understand why you don't like him. You spend a lot of time with the guy—for someone you don't like."

Momi was silent for a moment. How to explain without coming across as a total jerk? She sighed.

"The chemistry between us was always great. But it's what I mentioned to you before. I just can't see myself with someone who has no ambition at all. He speaks really well, so he's obviously educated. But he's content to have this nothing job and hang around the beach all day."

"Did you ask him why he took the job?"

"Not directly. And trying to weasel personal information out of him is just about impossible. The man is maddening."

"Momi, listen to yourself. You sound just like the heroine in a romantic comedy. I think you might be in love."

Instead of the wild denial Ruby expected, Momi moaned again. "I can hear you smiling," she grumbled. Irrational as the statement seemed, she knew her sister was smiling at her from her dorm room in Honolulu.

"You said he kissed you, so he must like you too. Maybe he even loves you."

But Momi wasn't going to fall for that. "You know guys don't have to be in love to kiss you."

There was a brief silence while they thought that over.

"The man can really kiss, though," Momi admitted.

"That's a good thing."

The sisters shared a laugh, talking for a while longer about the upcoming holidays, before they said good-bye.

Afterward, Momi sat, staring at her beautiful lilies.

Now what? Was it really love, this crazy, mixed-up feeling that gnawed at her belly?

Perhaps even more important . . . could she be with a man who was happy being an apartment manager? Or would his lack of ambition eat away at their relationship until she resented him? Did they even *have* a relationship?

And what would Great-great grandmother Helen think of all this?

As though by mutual consent, Momi and Rick managed to coexist for the next week without seeing each other except at a distance. Momi saw Rick on the beach when she left for work in the morning. Sometimes she glimpsed him there still when she returned at the end of the day.

Rick was aware of Momi's comings and goings. He seemed to have some type of radar when it came to her. He'd look over, and there she was.

It wasn't until Saturday morning that they once again came face-to-face. And in a very familiar way.

Momi knocked on Rick's door. Early.

As on that fateful Halloween night, Rick answered after a prolonged series of raps. As before, he was shirtless, his hair and body damp, his jeans pulled on and zipped.

"Oops." Momi's cheeks turned pink, and her throat went dry. "Déjà vu."

Rick's gaze went over her, from her head to her feet, and back again. "For déjà vu, you'd have to be wet too."

She winced. "Not today."

Momi stared into Rick's wonderful eyes. She had to make a real effort to pull her thoughts away from contemplating the beauty of his green irises. Because she had an important favor to ask.

"I hate to ask . . ." Momi began.

"Then don't." Rick started to close the door.

"Rick, wait." Her voice rose up to a near falsetto.

His face safely hidden behind the door, Rick smiled. He knew she was going to impose on him again. Yet he didn't mind. She was so cute when she got angry or excited. Besides, he'd spent the week trying to forget that kiss they'd shared. And unable to. It haunted him, even invading his dreams.

He composed his features before reopening the door. It wouldn't do to let her see his grin.

"What is it now?" He attempted to make himself sound like the curmudgeon he tried so hard to portray to his tenants. "Didn't we just do this last week?"

He saw her chest rise and fall as she took a deep breath. Then she smiled. It was almost impossible not to smile back when she turned on all that wattage. But he managed.

"Rick."

She wrung her hands—he'd never actually seen someone do that, just seen it described in books. But she held her hands at her waist, and they twisted around each other the entire time she spoke. Definitely wringing her hands.

"I'm in a spot. Again," she added before he could.

"What else is new?"

He pulled down one side of his mouth. Not quite a frown, but close enough to let her know he wouldn't be a pushover.

He could see the ripple of her throat as she swallowed; then she pulled out another devastating smile.

"I'm doing a story hour at the library later this morning. It's a special Christmas one that I've been planning almost since I started working there. The library employees have collected gifts for the underprivileged kids. I'd arranged for Santa to visit—the maintenance man at the library. But his wife just called."

Her voice rose in pitch again, to almost a whine. Tears clouded her eyes.

"He's having chest pains. She said he was having them all night and didn't tell her because he didn't want to go to the hospital and disappoint the kids this morning. But she convinced him to go to the hospital after all."

Momi managed a half smile. "She told him he would give all the kids nightmares if he collapsed right there at the party."

She was winding down. He knew what was coming,

and to his chagrin, it didn't bother him nearly as much as it should have.

"Rick, do you suppose you could . . ."

"You want me to play Santa?" he interrupted, his voice rising the same way hers had. Incredulous.

"Could you? Please?"

How could he even be considering such a thing? Rick Mahoney, the man who didn't do holidays. *Especially* Christmas. Playing Santa?

But Momi's eyes were full of sadness and pleading. He remembered the time she'd told him about her Good Night Story Hour, how her eyes had been so bright, he thought she'd probably enjoyed it as much as the kids.

Momi was still pleading.

"Do it for the poor, needy kids, Rick. Some of them might not get another present this Christmas, just what they receive this afternoon."

One more blink of those large, sad eyes and he agreed. He couldn't stand to see her so sad when it was in his power to help. Even if it did mean dressing up as Santa.

"I'll be a Hawaiian Santa, though," he told her. "I have a red Aloha shirt. I'm not wearing a fuzzy red coat or black boots."

He watched her agree happily, then trip back up the stairs.

Rick still couldn't believe he was doing this. Sitting in a room with a kid in his lap, another dozen waiting in line, and a fake beard irritating his neck and upper lip. He caught himself just before he sighed into the kid's ear. Why hadn't he thought of the beard when he'd stipulated about the coat and boots?

One small boy slid off his lap, and another, small and thin, climbed on.

"Hi, Santa."

This boy's voice was soft, his manner shy. Rick leaned in a little closer to be sure to hear him. There was something touching about this little guy. He had huge dark eyes, as dark as Momi's. His shirt was old and worn but clean and unstained. His pants were too short and patched at the left knee.

"If it's okay, Santa," he began, "I want you to bring my mama something this Christmas. I still have the truck you gave me last Christmas, and I play with it real nice, so it's still good. But Mama, she needs things she can use in the kitchen to make up supper. Sometimes we have to have cereal because she don't have the right pots to cook something nice. You think you could bring her something, Santa?"

His earnest eyes looked so trustingly into Rick's that his heart almost broke. Rick hated Christmas. He hated the commercialization, the decorations and sales that started two months prior, the attitude of greed he'd seen among the children of his associates. And in his wife. And he especially hated the way people tried to excuse bad behavior because "it's the holidays, after all."

But this poor child. He didn't even want anything for

himself. His truck was still good because he played carefully. A little guy like this shouldn't have to worry about playing carefully. With the junk they manufactured these days, his precious truck might break through no fault of his; then he'd blame himself and probably ruin his little life. It broke Rick's heart. Surely this child would make even the Grinch's heart grow two sizes.

"I'm sure we can do something about that. What's your name again?"

Catching his gaffe, Rick quickly did a hearty "Ho! Ho! Ho!"

"There are so many children in this world, you know, sometimes old Santa has to be reminded of their names."

The boy grinned at him, a sweet, trusting smile. "I'm Keanu Palama, Santa. And my mama's name is Liana Santos. We don't have the same last name, so I hope you don't get confused." His little mouth puckered in concern at this latest ripple.

"I think I've got it now," Rick told him. "Keanu Palama and Liana Santos."

Keanu smiled happily at him. Rick could see some of the other children looking restless. Keanu was taking up more of his time than the other children had, but he wanted to do this right.

"I've got a present here for you today, Keanu," Rick said, handing him the gaily wrapped package one of the library pages handed him. Momi had told him on the way in that there were two bags of toys, one red and one green. The red bag contained gifts for young girls and the green for young boys. There were further clues in the sizes and shapes of the packages. At the time, Rick thought the teen pages must all be Mensa members to remember the hints Momi provided about the packages.

Right now, Rick was sorry he hadn't paid more attention. He would have liked to know just what he was handing to Keanu in the beautifully wrapped green package. He hoped it was something really nice.

"Now, if I have some room in the sleigh and can include a little something extra for you, what would you like?"

The little boy's eyes widened as he looked between the new gift and the possibility of another.

Then his eyebrows drew together in concern.

"But you won't forget Mama, will you?"

"Nope. I won't. Liana Santos, right?"

Keanu grinned, and Rick felt his heart turn over. He suspected that the woman was a single mother who couldn't afford enough food to feed her son and used the absence of utensils as an excuse.

Looking at her little boy, Rick knew she must be a good person. She had to be, to raise such a precious child.

Keanu was smiling up at him, nodding vigorously.

"Yes," he agreed. "And if you do have extra room, Santa, I want a fire engine."

Beside Santa's chair, Momi heard Rick's conversation with Keanu, and her heart turned over too. She suspected that Rick planned to help them in some way, maybe supply a Christmas dinner and a toy for Keanu. He often tried to appear stern and gruff, but Momi knew he was a nice man. He was kind and cared about others.

As they returned to the apartment, Momi attempted to broach the subject. Besides, she wanted to help him help Keanu.

"Why don't you ever talk about yourself? Did you come here to escape something awful that happened on the mainland?"

As though the comment brought terrible possibilities to her mind, her eyes rounded, and her eyebrows rose. Then she gave her head a little shake. A grin tugged at the corners of her mouth.

"I was ready to suggest that you might be a fugitive from justice. But you aren't the type. You could never hurt anyone. And I can't picture you with a gun trying to rob a bank, either."

Momi recalled the gentleness of his manner with the children, especially his sincere concern for little Keanu and his mother.

But Rick, instead of being flattered by her impression of him, frowned at her. "Well, insult me, why don't you?"

Momi was startled by such a reaction.

"I beg your pardon?"

"And you should," Rick said. "You insulted me," he insisted. "Being a fugitive has a certain macho appeal, you know. Romantic, even. Think of that movie with Harrison Ford, the poor wronged soul, trying to find his wife's killer. It's almost as cool as James Bond."

Mimi was startled. Was he joking with her? Sometimes it was hard to tell. Could he really be insulted because she didn't think he had it in him to be a criminal? Men!

Rick had to work hard not to laugh. Momi was trying so hard to figure him out, and now she couldn't decide if he was kidding or not. He could almost read her thoughts as the changing expressions passed over her face.

Finally she set her mouth and shook her head. Decisively.

"You might like to imagine you're a dangerous person, but deep inside you're a pussycat. Besides, you're too smart to come to an island if you were a fugitive. Nowhere to escape if they come after you."

He looked at her for a moment before nodding. "Okay. I guess that's complimentary after all."

"Of course it is. At first I didn't think you were very bright." She watched as his eyebrows shot up. "The plumbing fiasco, you know."

If he wasn't trying so hard to be manly, she thought he might be wincing.

"But we've become friends since then, and I know you're not only kind but intelligent too. The only thing I can't figure out is why you're content to waste yourself working as an apartment manager."

His expression closed up, and Momi put a hand up, palm outward.

"I know, I know." Frustration threaded her words. "None of my business."

She sighed.

"So, what are you going to do for Keanu? And may I help?"

Rick's expression softened. The sweet little boy had gotten to him, just as he must have touched Momi.

"I'd like to give Keanu and his family a Christmas to remember. A bag or two of groceries so they can have a nice dinner. And those pots and pans he's so eager to give his mother. Some staples for later. A fire engine," he added with a grin.

Momi was nodding, her whole body thrumming with excitement. Her eyes sparkled, and Rick would not have been surprised to see her bouncing up and down with joy.

"That's just what I was thinking," she said. "Maybe our apartment house could adopt them, and we could all contribute. Get a tree, some ornaments, some clothing."

"Uh, maybe." Rick was wary. That kind of involvement would probably end his careful emotional distance. While it sounded good now, would he regret it next month?

"I'm sure Auntie Ruth would love to contribute something. She loves to sew and is always making things for her grandchildren. I'll bet she could make matching shirts for Keanu and his mother. And Ike works at KTA. Maybe he can get some of the groceries contributed, or get management to offer them a gift certificate."

Rick shook his head slowly from side to side. Momi had lived in his apartment building for less than six months. How did she know all that about the other tenants? He did know that Ike worked at KTA. Place of employment was something he felt the landlord ought to know. But he did not know that "Auntie" Ruth liked to sew. He tried not to get too involved with tenants, and that meant exchanging only the most general conversation.

"I'm going to make cookies for them," Momi declared. "That will be my contribution. Christmas cookies," she elaborated. "And maybe some gingerbread men. Those turned out well."

She looked over at him, her eyes filled with plans, with fun, with caring. With love.

Rick shook his head. Was he imaging things? Reading what he *wanted* to see in her expression, instead of what was truly there?

"Want to help?" Momi asked. When he stared at her, uncomprehending, she added, "With the cookies."

It wasn't until Rick agreed that Momi remembered her dream. Baking Christmas cookies with a man she loved. Flushing at the memory, she told herself that her tiny apartment kitchen was nothing like the bright, airy space of the dream.

She shook off the memory, trying to concentrate on reality.

"I'll borrow cookie cutters from my mom. My sisters and I used to bake cookies together with her when we were little. But as we got older, we were all involved in so many activities, there never seemed to be time."

Momi's enthusiasm did not diminish with her listing of various tasks. She continued to bubble over with plans.

"I could do up some flyers for the building, with a sign-up sheet. That way we'd all know what everyone else plans."

"Can you get information on Keanu from the party?" Rick asked. "I assume there was some kind of sign-up so that you would know how many to expect. Or would that not be allowed?"

Temporarily subdued, Momi quickly recovered. "I'll speak to the director. He'll know what's allowed. Maybe I can contact Keanu's mother and arrange something with her. Don't worry, I won't spoil the surprise. I could tell her that someone heard his request to Santa and wants to bring him a gift. Maybe I can get some clothing sizes from her too."

"Actually, that's an excellent idea. It wouldn't do to turn up there and have her get angry because she doesn't want charity."

Momi agreed.

And so the apartment building mobilized.

Within a week, various other tenants had signed on to help out. Momi talked over their plan with the library director and was given the okay to contact Keanu's mother from the party sign-up sheet.

"Be discreet," he advised. "Sound her out. We don't want to offend her."

Chapter Eleven

So it happened that Momi and Rick got together to bake Christmas cookies on the Friday before Christmas. She'd been in touch with Keanu's mother, who was moved to tears when she heard that someone wanted to help her son. And she provided all of her son's clothing sizes, confiding to Momi that he was in desperate need of pants and shoes for school.

Momi made up flyers for the apartment house bulletin board, and she and Rick already had a bagful of items as they began to mix the cookie dough. Auntie Ruth sewed up three Aloha shirts for Keanu and was working on a muumuu for Liana. Red, for Christmas, Auntie Ruth said, and in the same fabric as one of Keanu's shirts. Other tenants had contributed shoes and pants.

The weather had been ideal, with warm, sunny days followed by cool nights. Most evenings brought some showers, and Momi was religious in spritzing her fresh decorations, so they were still hanging along the stairwell, green and beautiful. Rick admitted getting compliments on the building's décor—all enthusiastic.

Momi found herself working to hide a grin. "So, there weren't any objections from those who don't celebrate Christmas?"

Rick shrugged. "I told you I don't like Christmas."

"But you've never said why." Momi sighed. "I don't want to pry. I just want to learn more about what makes you the way you are."

She saw his eyes going blank, the way they did whenever she attempted to get him talking about his past.

"It's what friends do, you know. They care about each other, and they listen to each other's problems."

"I never was one for friends," Rick said. Then he changed the subject.

"Why can't we make chocolate chip cookies?" He looked at the rolling pin and cookie cutters she had spread out on the counter, his eyes wary. "They're easy. You just spoon them onto the cookie sheet."

"Because chocolate chip cookies aren't as festive as Christmas cookies at this time of year. I want to make Christmas trees and Santas and stars and reindeer." She picked up cookie cutters of the various shapes as she spoke.

Rick shook his head. "Kids like chocolate chip."

Momi laughed. "Men do too. If you're a good boy, I'll make some for you later."

"It's a deal."

As they gathered the ingredients together, Momi couldn't help recalling her dream. The apartment kitchen wasn't large and bright like the one she'd seen. But she recognized the feeling of peace as they worked together.

Much as she'd denied it earlier, she was now convinced that Rick was the man her ancestor had found for her. She liked him, enjoyed spending time with him; she admired the way he'd reacted to Keanu's story, the way he'd moved immediately to help. He'd been there for her whenever she knocked on his door, too, even at awful hours of the morning.

She could see past his gruff exterior now, recognize that it was his way of keeping people at bay. He must have had a horrible experience somewhere along the way to make him this way. And his statement that he was "never one for friends" was heartbreaking. Momi wished he would open up to her. Because she felt sure that this concern she felt, the happiness in his presence, was love.

Rick's disgruntled voice interrupted her thoughts.

"Where's the butter? Cookies are supposed to have butter in them."

He was scanning the recipe she'd provided, inserted neatly into the binder he'd given her.

"I got this recipe off the Internet. It's supposed to be good for children. It has vegetable oil in it instead of butter."

Rick frowned at her. "It's Christmas. The kid should be able to have butter in his cookies. Did you try these?" He snapped his finger against the paper. "Do they have any taste?"

Momi looked stricken. "I just wanted to get the best recipe for a child. A healthy one." She moved to stand beside Rick and flipped to the next page in her folder. "I did ask my mother for her recipe. We could use this one."

His eyes quickly scanned the page. "Ah, real butter and sugar. And you turned out well. Let's use this one."

Momi brightened quickly. "I got these things to decorate them. If you'll roll the dough and cut out the shapes, I'd love to do the decorating with the icing and stuff."

He noted that her "stuff" seemed to include lots of little tubes and jars of colorful sugars and sprinkles.

"Fine with me. I'm not the most artistic person around."

"Okay. I'll cream the butter and sugar, and you can mix it after we put in all the flour. That's when it takes more muscle," she added with a wink.

She took the butter from the refrigerator, putting it into the microwave to soften.

"So, what are you then? If you're not artistic, I mean."

She measured out the sugar, getting it ready to add to the butter.

"I guess I'm a regular guy," he said. His tone did not invite any further questions.

As Momi packed the cooled cookies into a tin later that night, she couldn't resist looking back on her day. How wonderful it had been! She always had a good time cooking with Rick, and baking cookies had been no exception. It was nice that Rick could spend time with her on her days off; with the library schedule to consider, those free days were seldom on the weekend, which was their busiest time.

She took a last fond glance into the tin before adding a sheet of waxed paper and covering it. The cookies were beautiful and festive. She was sure Keanu would enjoy them.

Momi smiled as she thought back over the morning. Rick had had as much fun as she did, rolling out the dough and cutting out the shapes. Decorating them took a lot of time, but he had plunged right into the cleanup while she worked at applying the frosting and colored sugars. And he'd suggested starting a batch of gingerbread while she finished with the sugar cookies. He didn't complain about decorating those, helping her add the cinnamon "eyes" and raisin "buttons" without a qualm.

She sighed happily as she took a final glance around the neat kitchen. It might not be the large, sunny room of her dream, but it was a nice room and more than enough for her needs. Best of all, this afternoon she'd felt that same peaceful, loving atmosphere that had pervaded the dream.

She took a deep breath, holding it in as she admitted what the afternoon had made her realize. She was in love with Rick Mahoney. Ruby had been right all along. She'd met Rick right after she got the quilt. She just couldn't imagine them as a couple, not until today. Today, she realized how well they suited each other. And they worked well together—just look at how much she'd enjoyed cooking with him, decorating her gift tree, and even chaperoning the children on their field trip.

With a deep sigh, she turned off the light and retreated to her bedroom. If only she knew how he felt about her. He was so closemouthed about personal things, there was no way for her to know. She liked to think he enjoyed their time together as much as she did. And that was what had started the process for her. Would their continued friendship lead him to love as well?

"Rick, I'm glad I saw you."

Momi approached Rick from the direction of the laundry room. He held a rake and a black garbage bag, the latter puffed out and lumpy. "Been cleaning the atrium?"

"What was your first clue?" he asked.

She dismissed his smart remark with a wave of her hand.

"I want you to come to Christmas dinner with my

family. You shouldn't have to spend Christmas day here alone, and you've already met most of my family."

"Your sister Ruby going to be here for Christmas?"

She gave him a big smile. "Yes. The whole family will be together."

"Don't tell me. You've never spent a Christmas away from your family."

Momi seemed surprised that he would even ask. "Of course not. Christmas is definitely family time. My parents and Jade and her husband will be with us, but it's still a smaller group, not like Thanksgiving."

Her eyes brightened as she continued. "Did I tell you that Jade is pregnant? I suspected that was why they wanted to have Mom and Dad with them for the holiday—for Thanksgiving, I mean. They announced it then. I'll have my first niece or nephew in June."

"I'm happy for you," he said. "But no thanks for Christmas; I'd rather not." He wasn't rude, just definite. He'd already told her how he felt about holidays, and Christmas in particular.

Momi, however, wasn't ready to accept his answer.

"Don't be silly. Of all days not to be alone, I'd say Christmas ranks right up there at the top. You have to come with me. Being alone on Christmas would be even worse than being alone on Thanksgiving."

The pleading in her tone was just this side of whining. Why was she so anxious that he spend Christmas with her? Did she care more for him than he thought?

"Momi, I'll be fine. I like spending Christmas alone."

Momi didn't believe him, not even for a minute. Nor even a nanosecond. No one would *choose* to be alone on Christmas.

Rick deposited the garbage bag in the Dumpster and put the rake back into its place in the small locked closet beside it, where he kept his tools. He hoped Momi would give up and leave before he finished, but deep down he knew she would not.

She was still with him when he headed back to his apartment to wash up, still trailing along in his footsteps, the same earnest do-gooder expression on her face.

"I just don't like Christmas," he told her. "Okay?"

But she continued smiling at him in her "sure, tell me another" way. "Yes, you do. You just try to make everyone believe that you don't. I saw the way you were with little Keanu. You're seeing to it that he has a Christmas to remember. And you brought me a Christmas tree! If you hated Christmas that much, you would have thrown that tree into the trash and not cared about anyone else's reaction. And you wouldn't have played Santa for the library party or cared about a child's Christmas."

She shook her head. "No, you'll never convince me that you hate Christmas. You might pretend to be Scrooge, but you aren't. Not in your heart." Her voice was soft and gentle, her expression the same.

Rick looked at her. His expression was somber. It might be time to share his story. He wondered if she would be disgusted, as he had been. He'd separated himself from his only relatives because of what had happened. Would she withdraw from him after she heard it? He hated to admit how much he dreaded the possibility, but telling her was the only way he could think of to get her to leave him alone until December twenty-sixth.

"Come on," he said, taking her by the arm and leading her into his apartment. "I have a story to tell you."

Momi was used to Rick's abrupt tone but not the soberness of his expression. Had he ever been that serious with her? She was also curious about his apartment. In almost two months of friendship, she'd never stepped inside his place, just seen what was visible from the doorway. Which was very little. He had an attractive carved wooden screen angled just beyond the door that provided him with privacy. She'd seen him many times in his doorway talking to tenants, so she wasn't the only one who was left standing outside when reporting a problem.

As they stepped around the screen, Momi stopped short, pulling Rick up with her. His apartment was gorgeous! Who would have guessed that the beach bum manager had such a beautiful place? No wonder he kept that screen in position. It wouldn't do to have the tenants realize how much nicer this apartment was than any of the others.

Being just beneath her place, the main room of his apartment was the same size as hers. But it was furnished in such a way that it appeared much larger. For one thing, there was no counter separating the kitchen from the living area, just an island that encouraged the feeling that it was all one large room. As he'd told her after her disaster, he had the same white tile she did. His furniture was modern, lots of chrome and glass. But the chairs and sofa had large, comfortable-looking black cushions, and there was a large round rug, white and fuzzy as a polar bear. Although there were no photographs, there were some books and magazines, which gave the room a lived-in feel and saved the place from looking like a magazine spread. A huge modern painting hung behind the sofa, a swirl of blues and greens that somehow evoked waves and the ocean.

"This is beautiful," she said.

Rick shrugged. "I did some redecorating after I moved in."

"Can you do that in a rental?"

He didn't answer. He waved her toward the seating area and went to the sink to wash his hands. He didn't speak again until he returned with two juice cans and made himself comfortable.

"You like the *lilikoi,* right?" he said, offering her the can of passion-fruit juice. He opened the guava for himself.

She nodded to thank him, but she knew he didn't notice. He was deep into himself, and she knew his thoughts were not happy ones.

"I have a story to tell you," he said again. "Do you think you could just listen and not interrupt?"

He was so serious, Momi quickly agreed.

"I can tell from the way you look at me that you wonder why I don't have a better job."

Momi didn't deny it, but she did look embarrassed.

"Well, I used to have a very good job," Rick said. "For years, I was a workaholic. I had the big house, the trophy wife, and an imported sports car in the garage."

Momi gave a small start. He had a trophy wife? Something intangible wrapped around her heart, and a twinge of pain shot deep. As she dragged more air into her lungs, she concentrated on listening. She didn't want to miss any part of his story.

"I started a computer software company when I was in college, and it took off. I'd been a computer nerd for years, and a project I did for a class seemed like such a good idea, I decided to run with it. I was still in college when one of the computer magazines did an article about my company. Suddenly I had offers from all over the world. I was a hot property, and not only for headhunters. Women from the campus and beyond were approaching me for dates. And, uh, other things."

Momi almost laughed at the way his face became suffused with color.

"It was pretty heady stuff for a computer nerd who didn't even have a steady girlfriend. There isn't much time for things like dating when you're running a million-dollar company from your dorm room."

Momi looked suitably impressed. He'd always known she would be, if she heard his story. But would she like the man he'd become as much as the one he'd been?

"Lots of larger companies wanted to buy me out, but I hung on until graduation before accepting an offer—one that included an important position for me as part owner. I had to socialize for the job, and my partners intimated that having a wife to entertain for me would help with business contacts."

He took a deep breath, almost afraid to look Momi in the eye for this part.

"I was extremely foolish. I fell hard for a receptionist and part-time model I met in the elevator, of all places. Going to all those corporate meetings."

"She probably set you up," Momi said, forgetting her promise to just listen.

Rick nodded. "It took a long time for me to realize it, but I think you're right. We dated for a few months, and I asked her to marry me. We eloped—a weekend in Vegas. It was her idea." He ran his hands through his hair and wouldn't meet Momi's eyes. "But I still spent more time at the office than at home."

He took a long gulp of his juice.

"Then, on Christmas Eve night, three years ago, I came home around nine and found my wife and my stepfather making out in our richly appointed living room. I know it was richly appointed, because I paid the bills for the overpriced decorator my wife chose to do the work, who described it that way."

Momi may have been surprised when she heard he'd been married, but she gasped in shock when he mentioned what he'd discovered that Christmas Eve night.

Rick's eyes were gazing unseeingly at the coffee table. "We were supposed to have dinner with my mother and her husband, and I'd forgotten all about it. As usual. Elena had taken a cab over, thinking she'd drive home with me. When I didn't show up, dear old stepdaddy offered her a ride.

"And that wasn't even the worst of it," he told her. "No, the final blow was my dear mother's attitude. When I informed her of her husband's perfidy and told her I was getting a divorce as soon as my lawyer opened up his office after Christmas, my mother urged me to forgive them. 'After all, it's the holidays,' she told me. 'They must have had too much eggnog,' was how she put it. 'And gotten carried away under the mistletoe.'"

"Oh, Rick." Momi put a hand on his wrist. Tears welled in her eyes. Her voice was soft and gentle. "No wonder you don't like the holidays."

"The holidays were her justification. But I didn't see any reason someone could be a jerk on Christmas—or any other holiday—and be forgiven just because it's the season of good will."

He drank the last of his juice and crushed the can in his fist.

Momi smoothed her hand over his arm, taking the can from him before he cut himself on the sharp edges where the aluminum had cracked.

"My mother was my only family, and she cared more for her new husband—her new, young husband—than for her son." He closed his eyes for a moment. He thought he'd moved past the pain, but it was still there. And he didn't want to see Momi's pity.

But she surprised him.

"Well," she said, her voice brisk and practical. "That was three years ago, you said?"

He merely nodded, keeping his eyes closed and his head resting on the back of the sofa.

"Then it's time to move beyond it," she declared. "If you don't, then you're letting them win."

Surprised, Rick opened his eyes and sat up.

"What . . . ?"

He was practically sputtering.

"It's time you moved on and started celebrating again. You've made a nice start with Keanu and his mom," she continued, her voice firm. "You'll see. When we take everything over on Christmas Eve, you'll feel so great about the good you've done. You'll be filled with the Christmas spirit, the *true* Christmas spirit. You can make it a tradition—adopt a family every year. It will give you new Christmas memories—good ones."

She patted his arm again, unable to resist running her hand over his warm skin. "But how did you end up in Kona? I assume your company was on the mainland?"

Still staring at her, it took Rick a moment to gather himself together enough for an answer.

"Chicago. I threw Elena and my stepfather out of the house that night, locked all the doors, and spent the next twenty-four hours thinking. About my life, mostly. That was when I realized that I didn't have much of one. I spent all my time at work. Granted, I enjoyed my work, but I'd wanted children. Elena kept saying she wasn't ready."

Momi didn't say a word, but comfort flowed through her to him from the pressure of her small hand on his arm. He put his larger hand over hers and squeezed.

"I decided that awful Christmas that I was going to start over. I spent Christmas day packing all the things I wanted to keep—and there wasn't much. I decided to sell my interest in the business. My half of it was worth a great deal of money, though I had to share more than I wanted with Elena. Not half, though, because I'd already created the company and grown it before we got married. I'd been too much in love to ask her to sign a prenuptial. But it was all worth it."

Momi was being very patient with him. He still hadn't answered her question about how he'd arrived at a small apartment building in Kona, Hawaii.

"In working out the details of the divorce with my financial manager, I discovered that I had some investment property in Hawaii. It was December in Chicago, and Hawaii seemed like a good idea, so I headed over here for a vacation. I figured I'd have a look at the property, see if it was worth keeping."

Momi started. She was already ahead of him.

"Wait a minute. *You're* the landlord?" Her eyes drew together, and one side of her mouth pulled downward. "And you never told me? Even after we got to be friends?"

"I never told anybody in all the time I've lived here. You're the first person to know."

"But how could you live like this after the life you had?" She thought of workaholics she knew, tried to imagine them without their jobs. Impossible. Then she tried to imagine leaving her job and going off—to do what? Become a maid at a resort? That was the closest she could think of to what he'd done. She didn't think such a life would make her happy.

Busy with her thoughts, Momi didn't notice the anger and disappointment that filled Rick's countenance. He couldn't believe she was so focused on material things, but it looked as if she was. With her talk of family and its importance in her life, he'd hoped for better from her.

But her next words made him realize that he had misjudged her.

"How could you just give up the company you created? Go from working twenty-four/seven to relaxing on the beach?"

Relieved that she was thinking in terms of his work ethic rather than his material possessions, Rick shrugged. "I didn't want to do it anymore. All the hard work so that I could provide the best for my family. But I didn't have a family. At least, not the family I wanted— one of those rather old-fashioned ones, with parents and children who eat together every night and play games together. Much as I enjoyed my work, I'd initially seen it as a way toward an ultimate goal—the four-bedroom house in the suburbs with a swing set in the backyard.

Kids and a dog, maybe a cat too. But somewhere along the way, the ultimate goal was lost."

His voice trailed off, then strengthened again with his next sentence. Anger imbued his tone, even though it had been three years. "Instead of a family, children, all I had was a scheming gold digger for a wife, and a society woman for a mother. A society woman who was so afraid of losing her husband and therefore her place in her world that she wanted me to forgive him for something that I found totally unacceptable. I had to leave."

Momi nodded her acceptance. "I can see how you'd want a new start. But why not just start another division of your company in a new town?"

Rick shrugged again. There was no way he could communicate to her how he'd felt at the time—the betrayal, the depression, the disgust with everything in his life.

"It was a rough time for me. And then I came here." He looked around the apartment, his eyes taking in the cool, clean lines, and his chest filled with a satisfied warmth. "I looked at the apartment building, and I could see that it was old and needed work. But I fell in love with the location. I loved the sea air, the sound of the surf coming in through my window at night. I liked the young people I met on the beach. I think most of them were just on vacation, but I liked what they had. They had happiness, something I realized I had lost somewhere along the way to success. I had enough money to last the rest of my life, and I didn't have to work at all.

So I decided to take over the manager's job here, fix the place up myself. I wanted to become just a regular Joe."

He looked proudly around his apartment. Rick liked what he'd done with the place, and he'd done it all himself. It had taken a full year for him to get the rooms just the way he wanted. But he'd enjoyed the work of his hands, and he was happy.

Well, he had been happy, until Momi came into his life. Now he was unsettled. He'd sworn he'd never marry again, but he was so attracted to Momi that he was beginning to think about a family again. About a wife, and children, and a nice house. She was nothing like Elena. Perhaps now he really *could* achieve that old dream.

Momi was smiling. "I thought you were a beach bum. I couldn't figure out why you had such a great vocabulary when you acted like a high-school dropout."

Rick laughed. It felt good to let it all out. Maybe he'd be able to *really* put it all behind him now.

"So this is your chance for a new start, Rick," Momi continued. "We'll take the gifts to Keanu on Christmas Eve, and then you can come with me to my family's. We go to church at midnight. It starts the day off properly. You'll be making new memories. If you close yourself up in here all alone, you'll just spend the day brooding, remembering what happened. You *have* to do something new."

Rick met her eyes and was soon lost in them. How could such a young woman be so smart?

He sighed. "Okay. You've got me there. I suppose you're using your child psychology on me, or something."

Momi grinned. "Or something," she agreed. "So you'll come?"

"Okay."

"Great." She leaped up from the sofa. "I'll call and tell Mom to expect one more."

Chapter Twelve

Momi felt sure she would remember that Christmas Eve forever. Not because it was her first with Rick, though that was another memorable aspect of it. No, it was the special feeling of love that filled her heart that night and made her remember the true meaning of Christmas. It sounded trite when she told others about it later, but she knew it was because no words were adequate. You had to be there to recognize how truly notable the day was. As good as it had felt baking cookies with Rick earlier, giving the cookies away was ten times more fulfilling. The smiles—and tears—of the tiny family affected her far more than she had imagined.

Momi and Rick arrived at Keanu's door shortly after sunset. They were laden with gifts, hoping Liana would not be offended and feel they had gone overboard. There was a fire engine Rick had purchased for Keanu, the pots the boy had requested for his mother, the clothes made by Auntie Ruth and more donated by the other tenants. There were also other age-appropriate toys and games provided by some of the apartment residents— everything beautifully wrapped to go under the tree, which they also provided. In speaking to Liana earlier, Momi had discovered that they used a branch cut from a neighbor's juniper tree and stuck into a coffee can as their Christmas "tree." So Rick had gotten a lovely four-foot island tree—"nothing too ostentatious," Momi had advised—and Momi gathered together a "tree decoration kit" consisting mainly of gingerbread men and origami birds, with strips of paper already cut and ready to be made into a paper chain with the glue stick that was part of the supplies. Ike from the apartment building accompanied them, trailing behind with a cardboard box filled with groceries donated by his employer. It included all the makings for a traditional Christmas dinner, along with such staples as rice, canned soups, and peanut butter.

When he saw Santa at his door, Keanu's eyes opened so wide, Momi could see the white above the dark irises. His mouth rounded into a perfect *O*. Then, the first shock over, his mouth widened into an enormous grin, and his eyes sparkled with excitement. Behind him, Liana too smiled, but Momi could see the tears that filled her eyes.

"Look, Mama, look! Santa brought us a Christmas

tree!" Keanu tugged at his mother's hand until she was standing outside the front door too. The child looked ready to float into the air.

"Let Santa come inside, Keanu," Liana said, her hand on her son's shoulder pulling him gently back. "Can we get you some milk, Santa?" she asked.

Momi saw the startled look in Rick's eyes and almost laughed. This Santa might prefer a beer, she thought. But Rick did a nice save, even remembering to reply in the deep, hearty voice he'd affected for the children's party.

"Ho! Ho! Ho! Thank you very much, but Santa has a lot of work tonight, and he'll get lots of milk and cookies. So I'll pass on refreshments right now. Have to get a move on, you know."

He stepped inside, carrying the small tree, a bulging gift sack over his shoulder. For a moment, the sack caught against the door frame, and Momi had to help him by moving it toward the center of his back. Since her hands were full with the tins of cookies and the tree decorations, she managed the maneuver with her elbow. Behind her, Ike had his own problems maneuvering through the door with his arms overladen with the heavy box.

Santa set the tree in their small living room, then squatted down to be at Keanu's level.

"Santa would love to help you decorate this tree, but this is my busy day, you know. So you and your Mom will have to do it after I leave. Auntie Momi brought some decorations," he added, calling her by the name the children at the library used.

Keanu nodded solemnly, still awed that Santa had taken the time to stop off at his house on Christmas Eve.

"Thank you, Santa," he replied politely.

Behind him, his mother beamed at his correct manners.

Keanu's face became animated as Santa proceeded to empty out his sack, covering the floor space beneath the tree with gaily wrapped gifts. Liana's eyes filled with tears she could not suppress.

Keanu was overwhelmed as package after package came out of Santa's pack—gifts marked for both him and his mother.

"But what about the toys for the other boys and girls?" he asked, his gaze settling on the newly flattened red flannel bag lying on the floor. His small forehead furrowed in concern that his windfall might prove detrimental to others.

Momi wanted to hug the child—and his mother, who had obviously raised him right and in a less than ideal situation. She was also happy that Rick answered the question immediately.

"Ho! Ho! Ho!" he said. "Santa's sack is magic, you know. Only the toys for one house fill it each time. Otherwise, it wouldn't fit inside the door, much less the chimney." Rick/Santa smiled reassuringly at Keanu. "There are plenty of gifts for all the children in my sack."

Momi's heart felt ready to burst from her chest as she watched Rick interact with the child. His quick wit made him capable of answering the boy's questions immediately, with no long pauses to think of suitable replies. If she didn't know any better, she'd think he was the real Santa herself.

Afterward, the three gift bearers returned to the apartment house to tell the others who had participated in donating items all about it. Ike was eloquent in his praise of Rick's Santa and admitted to suppressing a tear or two at the happiness they had brought to the small family. Momi passed around a tin of cookies, and Auntie Ruth presented everyone with small tissue holders made from scraps of bright Hawaiian-print fabric. A shy young man who lived at the opposite end of the second floor provided everyone with "fish hook" pendants he'd created himself.

The gathering, which became a small celebration in itself, added to the serene happiness that filled Momi that evening. It was nice to get to know more of her neighbors and to see them interacting with one another. During the workweek, everyone was too busy to take the time to do more than wave.

Even with this impromptu get-together, Momi and Rick arrived at the Kanaheles' well before they had to leave for the midnight service. There was time enough to introduce Rick to those he had not yet met, to wish everyone a Merry Christmas, and to have eggnog and cookies before it was time to go to church.

As they visited over her mother's butter cookies, Momi once again told the story of Keanu and his Christmas. Rick was embarrassed by the praise he received for his part in the little drama, but Momi smiled at him with so much pride that he was able to set aside his discomfiture.

As they sat in the small church, Rick had to admit that the evening was nothing like any of his previous Christmas celebrations. There had been no unpleasant memories to remind him of the past because this island Christmas was a completely new experience. Here, there were no sophisticated parties where the women tried to outspend one another on the latest fashions. There were no businessmen trying to outdo each other with elaborate and exaggerated corporate tales.

Everything he and Momi had done to celebrate was something he'd never done before. Baking cookies with Momi, stringing popcorn. The gifts they'd organized for the small, struggling family, which had made him feel like he truly was Santa Claus. The love and caring that suffused the Kanahele family as they visited together before leaving for church.

Even this midnight service was unique.

Momi held his hand as they sang the familiar carols. Trade winds blew into the open windows of the church, and although it was past midnight, the temperature was mild compared to a Chicago winter's night. The smell of the sea air, the pots of poinsettias and orchids that decorated the altar, the island children dressed in traditional

Hawaiian costumes to enact their version of the nativity play—it was all new and wonderful.

And to think he'd been missing this for the past three years. Still, it wouldn't have been the same without Momi by his side.

Rick squeezed her hand, and she squeezed back without removing her gaze from the altar.

After the service, with the strains of "Silent Night" still lingering in the night air—and even that was a new experience, as they'd sung it in Hawaiian—Rick knew that he would be taking Momi's advice to start anew. Tonight would be the first of his new, happy holiday experiences. And it would be up to him to make sure all future holidays were equally fulfilling.

The spiritual warmth of the glorious night remained with Momi and Rick back at the apartment building as he walked upstairs with her. It was a beautiful night, with mild temperatures and brilliant stars overhead. It was also the most memorable Christmas of Rick's life. So when they reached her door, it seemed the most natural thing in the world to share a good-night kiss.

He began with a light and tender touch of his lips on hers. Just in case Momi did not feel the same way he did, he wanted to give her the opportunity to pull back.

But she did not. In fact, she leaned into him, pressing against his chest and threading her arms around his neck. Rick deepened the kiss, letting his lips draw hers open, running his tongue lightly over the fullness of her lower lip. He swallowed her sigh and pulled her even closer.

Rick didn't want to end the kiss. This night was so special, this woman even more so. She was his own special Santa: she'd given him back Christmas. With her whining and pleading, with her encouragement, with her support and all her help, he'd actually experienced a meaningful, incomparable day.

With a sigh of his own, he finally managed to pull away. But he continued to hold her close, cradling her head against his shoulder. They stood that way for what seemed a moment, for what seemed a day. Rick didn't know if any animals had spoken at midnight, but he would not have been surprised to hear that the old legend had become true this Christmas night. For tonight, anything seemed possible.

Rick put a hand over Momi's head, running his fingers lightly over her hair. Her unique fragrance tickled his nostrils, and he took a deep breath. The scent that had come to mean Momi to him.

"What is that perfume you use, Momi? Or is it your shampoo?" He breathed it deeply into his nostrils for a second time. "It's delicate and sweet, and whenever I smell it, I think of you."

Momi didn't move her head from his shoulder, just snuggled in closer, if that was possible.

"It's white ginger," she replied. "It's my soap and shampoo." Her voice was slightly muffled against his shirt, and she seemed almost breathless.

Rick considered this last and decided it was a fine thing. Another gift for him on this special night.

He moved his hand up and down over her back, enjoying the feel of her in his arms. Her presence there seemed so absolutely appropriate, it was downright scary.

And it was late—or, rather, early—on Christmas morning and past time they should part.

"Thank you for a beautiful evening, Momi."

Rick's words, though softly spoken, sounded loud and clear in the quiet night. It was going on two in the morning, and everyone else in the building seemed to be asleep. The apartment windows were all dark, the night indeed silent.

Her head still nestled against his shirt, Momi chuckled. Surprised, Rick leaned back enough to peer into her face. Her eyes sparkled, amusement and something deeper shining up at him.

"Shouldn't that be my line?" Momi asked.

Rick had to think for a moment before realizing that she referred to the traditional date ending, where the woman thanked the man before disappearing inside.

Rick smiled. "No. In this case it's definitely my line. You were right, Momi, and I never believed you could be. This day has been wonderful. Giving Keanu a Christmas to remember is one of the most fulfilling things I've ever done. And I found the service this evening moving. It's just barely Christmas day, and I've already had the best holiday of my life. I hate to admit how wrong I've been, ignoring, or trying to ignore, the season. But I think I'll finally be able to put aside those old memories now. Thanks to you."

Momi's smile widened, and she bent forward, kissing him impulsively once again.

But what started as an impetuous touching of her lips to his quickly turned into another soul-searing moment. As Rick deepened the kiss, he felt Momi respond, and his arms tightened around her once more. His entire body tensed with the strength of his reaction to this singular woman. Would he be able to manage anything without her?

It was the low moan pulled from Momi's throat that brought him back to reality. It was two o'clock on Christmas morning, and he and Momi should both be inside, tucked into warm beds, dreaming of sugarplums—whatever the heck they were.

With supreme effort, Rick released Momi and stepped away from her. Then he almost took her back into his arms when he saw her shiver. The sea air was cool, and he, at least, had just been superheated.

But he managed to keep his arms to himself and instead offered a sad smile. "Good night, Momi. Merry Christmas."

"Merry Christmas."

Momi's voice was stronger than she'd expected. After that devastating kiss, who knew she'd be able to speak at all?

Tempted to step close for another hug, for another good-night kiss, Momi somehow managed to remain where she was. Until Rick cleared his throat and asked if she had her key.

A nervous giggle escaped her throat. "My key. Right."

She stuck her hand into her purse, rummaging for the key ring. She was glad when Rick took it from her, his hand warm and gentle against hers. With the problems she was having concentrating, she wasn't sure she would have been able to open her own door. She certainly wasn't able to think.

But Rick was his usual competent self. Her door was soon opened, and she stepped inside. Reluctantly. As she gripped the edge of the door, easing it slowly closed, she looked back at her landlord. Had it really only been since Halloween that she'd known him? Sometimes it seemed like forever; sometimes it seemed like mere hours.

"Good night. See you in the morning?" They were supposed to leave for her parents' house around nine-thirty. Just hours from now.

Rick nodded, and Momi wondered if he, too, was having trouble controlling his voice. It didn't seem likely, she admitted, as she finally shut the door and turned the bolt. Rick was always so in control. He always seemed to know what he wanted, too, even if he wasn't always correct in knowing what that was.

Chapter Thirteen

During the week between Christmas day and New Year's Eve, Momi tried to keep herself too busy to think. Christmas had surpassed all her expectations. It was memorable not only for the warmth of `ohana, or family, on a special day, but because of her love for Rick. The kisses they'd shared early on Christmas morning had to be as important, as mind-bending, to him as they had been to her. Didn't they? When it came to Rick, her thoughts whirled in circular patterns, and she could come to no solid conclusions.

So she threw herself into library programming instead. She decided to do bulletin boards and programs on New Year traditions in the various cultures that made up the local island population. Such programming should have been planned months ago, of course, but she knew she could make it work. The library tended to be crowded with children in these vacation days, as their parents looked for something to keep them busy. So Momi could round up a crowd for impromptu programs involving not only the children, but their parents as well. Because she knew how to make the programs interesting. The branch director wasn't sure about such last-minute plans—not until he saw the enthusiasm of over a dozen adults and children creating a Chinese dragon from crepe paper. By the time it was ready to wind its way through the library and out into the parking lot, there were over two dozen exuberant patrons involved.

New Year's Day was uppermost in Momi's mind these days, not just at work, but at home. On Christmas Eve, Jade invited all of her family to the New Year's Eve party she and Adam would be hosting at the resort. As manager of the Orchid House Resort, Adam was responsible for entertaining their most important guests. Holiday guests often came back with their families year after year, and he tried to encourage such repeat business with lavish entertaining.

Three weeks ago, Momi wouldn't have been caught dead at such an affair with Rick. Now, after Googling his name, she knew that he would be more at home in such a setting than she herself. Momi didn't know why she hadn't thought to Google Rick earlier. Well, yes, she did. She hadn't thought the name of a beach bum in Kona, Hawaii, would lead her to anything—except possibly a MySpace page or a video on YouTube.

Though, as she thought about it, she wasn't sure she would have recognized the man she uncovered as the Rick Mahoney she knew. There were dozens of Richard Mahoneys, and two weeks ago she might not have been able to identify her new friend among the many. He looked different in his business clothes, too—younger, as surprising as that seemed.

And two weeks ago she certainly would not have believed that what she read there could possibly pertain to her apartment's manager. Richard Mahoney's business credentials were amazing. He had not only been highly successful, but well respected in his field. The winner of multiple awards. Praised for his innovation, not only in the software business itself, but for the comfortable working conditions he insisted on for his employees. He was one of the first to insist on day care and exercise facilities adjacent to the work space, and the break rooms provided healthy snacks at all times.

More than ever, Momi was amazed that he was able to leave it all behind so easily.

During her hours of busywork, trying to find enough information to keep up with her new and popular programs, a daring plan began to form in Momi's mind. A plan that would let her know once and for all how Rick really felt about her. The thing was—could she do it? At first, it seemed to go against everything she'd always held dear; but when it came down to it, she was pretty much of a nonconformist. Not in the way Rick was, dumping an important job and his whole lifestyle to set himself up as what appeared to be nothing more than a handyman. But she did hate to live according to arbitrary rules. And the more thought she put into her situation, the more it seemed that what she faced now was nothing more than that—an arbitrary system that said "this is how it should be, because it is how it's always been."

The more she thought about it, the more excited Momi got. She was going crazy waiting for something more to happen with Rick. Wondering if he felt the same way she did. Why not do something to get things going? It was the twenty-first century after all.

Besides, it was the only thing she could come up with.

Momi pushed aside all worries about her bold plan on Monday morning. Waking up beneath the heirloom quilt, she realized that she'd had another dream. A wonderful dream.

In it, she was sitting on the steps of a wide, old-fashioned porch. A large lawn stretched out beyond the porch, and small children played there. Beyond the yard she could see the ocean. And farther out still, in the turquoise waters, dolphins played. Dolphins, her family's `aumakua.

Momi smiled. She recalled the dream in such clear detail, she knew that her ancestor Helen was speaking to her. Her ancestor, out there in the ocean, watching over her in her dolphin guise. Because a man sat beside her on the porch, his arm around her, while they watched the children play. She could feel the love that embraced them and extended to the children.

And, this time, when she turned her head to look at the person beside her, she didn't wake up, nor was the person's face blurred. This time, she saw the man's face, a face that had become dear to her. Rick Mahoney. Grandmother Helen had chosen him for her after all. She'd have to apologize to Ruby.

Momi folded the quilt back carefully, then almost leaped out of bed. She felt refreshed and happy in a way she had not been for some time. Life was good. She was in love. And she was almost certain that everything would work out for her. *Almost* certain. She hoped Grandmother Helen's *mana* was powerful enough. But, just in case, her plan would help.

And so she strategized, mapping things out as carefully as she did for one of her children's programs.

First, she needed a killer dress—the most wonderful dress she could find—to wear to Jade's party. Red. She decided it had to be red. And red and slinky would be even better. She'd had no luck finding anything suitable over the weekend and worried that she might be too late to find what she wanted.

So she enlisted Jade and Ruby to help her shop.

"I need a dress that will knock Rick off his feet," she told her sisters.

Although they spent what time they could spare scouring shops, it was Jade who found the perfect dress—online. Then she tracked down a local store that carried it, and the sisters hurried there so Momi could try it on.

Once dressed, Momi stared into the three-way mirror, unable to say a word.

"You look beautiful!" Jade exclaimed.

"Wow!" was Ruby's succinct comment. Then she hugged Momi. "I knew this would happen," she said, releasing Momi and turning to Jade. "Back in November, I suggested that Rick might be the one the quilt brought to her, but would she listen?"

They all three laughed, but Momi continued to stare at herself in the mirror. This was it. This was the dress that would help her bring her daring plan to fruition.

She didn't tell her sisters about the plan, though. That was too private to share with anyone. She just let them know that she was in love. And that she needed to impress Rick.

Her dedication in searching out the perfect dress was rewarded when she saw Rick's face on New Year's Eve.

He knocked on her door at precisely the time agreed upon.

Momi was ready. Her wonderful dress, red and slinky, decorated with beads and lace—but, unlike the flapper dress, no fringe—emphasized every curve of her generous figure. She wore the strappy red sandals, too, which had survived the Halloween flood.

Rick stared. He stood still for so long, not moving a

muscle, she wondered if he might have stopped breathing.

Then he sucked in a huge breath and greeted her, his face solemn. "Momi. You look amazing."

She smiled. "*Mahalo,* Rick. You look pretty good yourself."

He wore a tailored gray suit—a suit!—something she never thought she'd see in person on the free-spirited Rick.

His lips quirked up on one side at her comment. "Haven't been this dressed up for years. I wasn't even sure the suit would still fit."

Momi looked him up and down, her greedy eyes taking in every detail. "I'd say it does," she told him.

With a chuckle, Rick took her sweater from her arm, holding it while she put it on. As she poked her arms into the sleeves, then drew the edges together at her chest, Rick leaned down and placed a kiss at a spot below her earlobe.

Momi shivered—and not from the cold. Her eyelids fell, suddenly heavy, and it took some effort to pry them open again.

She smiled at Rick as he put his arm around her waist and led the way to the door.

"It's going to be a wonderful evening," she murmured.

He didn't disagree.

The party was as good as she expected. Excellent food, marvelous company, a lively band. Rick even danced with her, and with her sisters and her mother. He apologized for his efforts, but Momi thought him quite tolerable as a dancer.

It was drawing closer to midnight when Jade caught her on her own, returning from a visit to the ladies' room.

"Your boyfriend is keeping my husband from his hosting duties," she complained.

But Momi could see that Jade wasn't the least bit angry. She actually smiled as she spoke.

Momi followed her sister's gaze to a corner beside the bar, where the two men appeared to be engrossed in a serious discussion. They stood, heads together, ignoring the celebration around them.

"What are they talking about, do you know?" Momi thought they seemed terribly solemn for such an entertaining party.

Jade put a hand on Momi's arm. "It's wonderful, Momi. I can see why you love him. Rick is talking to Adam about starting a charity foundation. He wants to call it Holiday Dreams, and it will help families with small children who find themselves in trouble at Christmastime. So that the kids can have a Christmas and not lose faith in Santa."

Momi felt tears gather in her eyes and blinked rapidly to hold them back. She didn't want to have raccoon eyes at midnight. That's when she would implement her plan, and she wanted to look her best. But, gosh, she loved that man! And this was such a fabulous idea.

But then a niggling doubt crept into her, causing a

flutter of fear in her midsection. "I wonder why he didn't ask *me* to help?"

Jade's merry laughter rang out, and Momi noticed Adam's head come up and his eyes unerringly meet his wife's.

"Because librarians don't have that kind of money to invest, silly. I'm sure he'll come to you when he needs help with the day-to-day stuff."

"Ah . . ." Momi blushed, and the sick feeling she'd had a moment ago smoothed into the slight nervous flutter of butterflies. Of course he'd need cash to get something like that off the ground. Serious cash, like the kind Adam's family of hoteliers would have to invest.

She felt her chest tighten with pride in the man she'd chosen to love. In the past two months she'd learned that he was special, but this would be proof to the rest of the world. If he let anyone know about his part in it, of course. It wouldn't surprise her in the least if he wanted his participation to remain anonymous.

As the minute hand drew inexorably closer to the twelve, couples who had scattered about the room drew together once more. At eleven fifty-five, the master of ceremonies signaled the waiters, who surged forward with trays of Champagne-filled flutes. He began the countdown at eleven fifty-nine and fifty seconds, and the crowd counted with him.

At midnight, they all raised their glasses to toast the

New Year. The band swung into "Auld Lang Syne," and Rick took Momi into his arms for a kiss.

Momi returned his kiss, trying to put all of her love into it.

They parted reluctantly, following everyone out to the lanai, where they could watch the fireworks exploding over the ocean. The resort had hired pyrotechnic specialists to create a show for their guests from a barge anchored offshore. Fireworks to welcome in the New Year was a time-honored tradition in Hawaii, brought in long ago by the islands' Asian immigrants.

Rick led her to a spot on the far side of the lanai, where they had some privacy away from the main body of guests. Momi leaned against him, sighing with pleasure. Rick responded to her sigh, pulling her even more snugly against him. They watched the colorful display in this way for several minutes before Momi pulled back enough to gaze up into Rick's face. She watched the colored lights play across his countenance—the face that had become so dear to her.

It was time to put her plan into action.

"Rick." Her lids closed nervously over her eyes before opening fully. She stared into his eyes, willing him to feel the same way she did. "We're good together, don't you think? We should get married."

There. She'd done it. Her plan. A proposal of marriage. Why should the guy always have to do the asking?

Rick looked down into her face, staring silently for a moment before breaking into laughter.

Momi pulled away from him, slapping at his pecs in frustration as he held on to her arms, refusing to let go.

"Are you laughing at me? You're terrible!"

She tried to turn away from him, not wanting him to know that tears were seeping into her eyes. She'd be mortified if he saw her cry. But he wouldn't let her leave.

"Momi." He'd stopped laughing but was still smiling broadly. "I'm not laughing at you. It's me! I'm such a fool."

He gave her a swift kiss, right on her lips, then pulled her back even more into the shadows. Then he freed one hand long enough to reach into his pocket.

"I brought this with me tonight. I've been carrying it around for a week now."

He held up a small jeweler's box, white velvet. The type of box that usually held a ring.

"I wasn't sure you'd want me. I know I've become a lonely old curmudgeon these past few years. So I kept putting off asking if you wanted to marry me, because I was afraid you might turn me down. And then you beat me to it!" He shook his head, still chuckling.

"You were going to ask me?" Momi grinned, joy filling her entire face. "So then you think we should get married?"

"Definitely." Sober now, Rick nodded solemnly. "I love you, Momi."

Momi was serious too. "I love you too, Rick."

Another kiss was called for, one that lasted a bit longer. As they drew apart, Rick spoke. "Let's make it official." He opened the ring box and showed her what it contained. "Do you like it?"

Momi's eyes widened as she looked at the ring. It was a perfect pearl, smooth and round and opalescent, and surrounded by sparkling diamonds.

"Ohhh!"

"Wow," Rick said. "I can't believe it. I think I made you speechless. Definitely a first."

Momi was too delighted to be offended. Her fingers fluttered over the ring. She wanted to take it from the box, wanted to see it on her finger. But, unaccountably, she found herself suddenly shy.

"Rick." His name came out on a puff of breath. "It's so perfect."

"I know."

He smiled, looking so smug and happy with himself that Momi frowned at him. But she couldn't be mad at him, not when he'd just said her loved her. And the ring *was* perfect.

"It had to be a pearl for you, Momi. You're my pearl." Rick shook his head. "And I can't believe I said something so corny."

He gave her a tender smile as he took the ring from its velvet nest and slipped it onto her left ring finger.

"Now it's official," he said. "Let's go tell your family."

"Yes." Momi held her hand against his chest, fingers spread, so that she could admire the beautiful ring. Over the ocean, the fireworks continued to glitter and sparkle, making her new ring glow pink, then gold, then ivory in the changing light. Momi sighed with pleasure.

"But first . . ." She pulled his head down. "First, another kiss," she suggested.

Rick happily obliged. As her eyes closed, Momi realized there were stars dancing in the sky behind them. Showers of stars. It was so right. She remembered how she'd hoped for bells ringing and stars exploding when she first met her "true love." Then she'd been disillusioned by Jade's story. But now she was getting her stars.

And as her eyes closed, she heard horns and whistles, and she realized that the party guests were making use of the noisemakers provided by the hotel. Not quite bells, but totally appropriate.

As Rick's lips closed over hers, she felt the magic of the moment. This was a night she would never forget.